# A Dangerous Bargain

## BOOK ONE

### The Sentinel Demons

J. S. Scott

A Dangerous Bargain
(The Sentinel Demons)

Copyright © 2013 by J. S. Scott

Cover Design by Cali MacKay - Covers by Cali
Edited by Faith Williams - The Atwater Group

ISBN: 978-1-939962-41-6 (paperback)
ISBN: 978-1-939962-33-1 (ebook)

*This one is for all of my incredible friends who have supported my writing and who bring me so much joy every single day: Melissa, Clara, Judy, Cali and Rita. I'm grateful to have such strong, supportive and awesome women as friends. You girls rock!*

*-J.S.-*

# Content

# Prologue

*"The Sentinel Demons-A History"*
AUTHOR-UNKNOWN

*M*any people believe that demons are evil spirits, possessing humans, taking over their minds and bodies until they are nothing but a shell, a vessel for the evil entity that dwells inside them. What most humans don't know is that there are also other types of demons, physical beings created thousands of years ago, during a period of time when demons came to rule the Earth, having been set loose by careless gods who used them for chaos and revenge. The gods created them in so great a number that they finally had to confine all their creations to a demon realm, a prison that could contain them. Said gods, who are now considered nothing more than myth, and whose vanity was endless, adamantly refused to destroy the demons-to annihilate all of them would be an admission that what the deities had done was actually wrong. All-powerful, all-knowing gods and demigods did not make errors. They themselves declared it impossible. And how could they destroy their own magic, lose creatures that might be needed later? After all, the gods were usually at war, and what if they needed their evil creations for weapons? So instead, the demons stayed *confined to the demon realm, a place where no god would venture-a realm of such vile evilness, such toxicity and so malodorous, that no selfish deity could tolerate visiting.*

*The realm was hidden, situated between Earth and Hades, a place where the demons remained, multiplied, and grew in strength while the gods ignored their existence. Unfortunately, ignoring such heinous immortals eventually created utter chaos, the demons finally gaining enough power to leave the demon realm and create havoc on an Earth that was, by that time, inhabited by a large population of humans. These demons became known as the Evils.*

*Devastation ruled, humans being taken in large numbers, disappearing in droves. The balance between good and evil tipped, evil ruling the planet, creating a rift that not even the gods themselves could fix. Desperate to restore sanity to an insane world, the gods tried in vain to destroy the vile beasts that upset the equilibrium, finally putting aside their vanity in favor of survival. But it was too late; the demon population was too large, too powerful, and the egotistic gods weren't about to venture near the Evils to destroy them.*

*Desperate, the deities banded together and created a new breed of demon to fight the Evils; the newcomers' souls would still be dark, but their purpose would be to protect humans from becoming extinct, bringing good and evil back into balance. These newly-created Sentinel demons blended in, appearing human...but they weren't. They were magical beings, although they adapted and took on more facets of humanity as they evolved. Having given the guardian demons the power to recruit humans and thus replace Sentinels lost in the battle between good and evil, the gods no longer needed to be bothered with their "annoying little problem" and went to war with each other once again, losing power as the centuries passed and humans ceased to worship them. However, the Sentinels carried on, striving to protect the human population, governing themselves and growing in magical powers, even though the gods had embedded a set of rules into the Sentinels' magic-supposed fail-safes imposed to keep the guardian demons in check. Still, the Sentinels brought balance back to the planet in spite of the stifling rules, finding ways to bend them or work around them, angry that the only rule imposed on the Evils was that human victims could not initially be taken by force, or coerced via lies. But manipulation was easy for an Evil, and once a human had agreed to an Evil's bargain, there was no end to the torture the heinous demons could impose upon the duped individual in order to increase their own strength.*

*So…are all demons evil? They are all dark at their core, and have some degree of inherent wickedness…but demons were not all created equal.*

*Evils and Sentinels are both demons, engaging to this day in a battle of good versus evil that has been going on for thousands of years, a war that most humans are blissfully unaware even exists. However, for the small percentage of individuals who actually have encounters with demons…their lives will never be the same.*

Kristoff Agares, king of the Sentinel demons, placed the anonymous papers back into a manila folder with a sigh, dissolving the whole file into thin air with a single mental command. When he had first started getting reports about a human writing about his people, he had blown it off. Most of the sparse information about the Sentinels coming from human origins was mere speculation or myth, not a threat to the existence of his brethren. However, the person writing these accounts was getting too close to the truth for comfort and needed to be stopped. He had a pretty good idea who was authoring the information, and that person had enough dirt about the Sentinels to be dangerous. Fortunately, he knew exactly how to handle the situation, and, if his suspicions were correct, the outcome was bound to be entertaining.

He smiled as he teleported himself from his stately home in Seattle to another equally impressive residence on the Olympic Peninsula, located in an area where humans were few and far between. The residence was more of a palace than a home, hidden from hikers or anyone who might happen to pass by the remote area, by the magic of the gods-or rather, the magic of a goddess, the only one still powerful enough to remain on Earth, while all the others had faded away to the kingdom of the dead. Personally, Kristoff secretly believed the majority of them belonged in

Tartarus, rather than Elysian Fields, for creating the Evils and bringing so much suffering to so many humans with their selfishness. As far as he knew, this particular goddess was the only one who had argued against the gods' folly of creating, and then ignoring, the Evils, which had allowed them to eventually overrun the Earth.

*What would I do without Athena?*

Honestly, Kristoff didn't want to find out. The female deity was his advisor, his confidante, and Athena gave new meaning to the expression of having a "longtime friend" since they had known each other for thousands of years. There were moments when he needed the insight and wisdom of the fragile goddess, and now was one of those times. She had summoned *him*, but he had already sensed that change was coming.

*I just wish I had a little more clarity.* It really irritated the hell out of him when he didn't have complete information.

"Athena?" he called loudly, his booming voice echoing in the opulent residence. He had materialized in her monument room, a large hall filled with statues of the Greek gods. Scowling as he passed marble statues of Apollo, Artemis, and Zeus, he shook his head, grateful that only Athena remained. The rest of them hadn't been worth a shit, and he couldn't bring himself to regret that they were gone, although he knew that Athena still missed some of her family. Exiting the room, he made his way down a grand spiral staircase. The steps were made of gold, the sparkle glinting from the tiles-probably diamonds and gemstones. The residence was ostentatious, and personally, Kristoff cringed at the gaudy furnishings, from the crystal chandeliers to the heavy forest green draperies, but he knew that Athena didn't decorate this way for show. After all, who came to visit except him? No...Athena did what she thought was pretty and cheerful, money really having no meaning to her. She obviously liked the flashy décor, and was able to manifest anything she damn well pleased to try to brighten her solitary existence.

Kristoff knew Athena was lonely because he knew exactly what it was like to be isolated. Cut off, different...and always alone. But at least he had his Sentinels, even if he couldn't always share everything with them. They were amusing and good company-when he didn't feel like bashing their heads together for doing something stupid.

Athena was sequestered here, her existence known only to him, a prisoner of the grand residence she had created in this isolated area. If she wandered far from her residence, she became sick, confused, and unable to function; thus, she was confined to this area, unable to travel far from her home without some very adverse effects on her body and mind.

Kristoff found her in the solarium, surrounded by lush green plants that she was currently watering with a serene expression that instantly calmed him. Athena was balance and enlightenment, and although she might not always have the answers to his questions, her aura was tranquil and soothing. Not that the goddess didn't have a temper that could be fearsome, but her core essence was peaceful.

"Kristoff!" she exclaimed as she turned, her watering pot disappearing from her hands as her face formed a brilliant smile. "Thank you for coming."

He nearly laughed. Athena had summoned him, and he would have to be a complete idiot to ignore the summons of a goddess, but she greeted him like an unexpected guest. "You called me," he reminded her, making himself at home as he sat down on one of the chairs perched around a small glass table.

She moved toward him gracefully, looking almost fragile. Although there were many depictions and likenesses of the Greek goddess of wisdom-Athena-none of them was totally accurate. She was slight, with her long silvery blonde hair currently in a braid down her back, her slim figure dressed in a flowing silky blue robe that was several shades darker than her ice-blue eyes. Reaching the table, she seated herself elegantly across from him. "Yes. I requested your presence, but I didn't know when to expect you," she answered in her soft, melodic voice. "The time for the Sentinels to increase their magic is coming soon, and it's imperative that they do so because the Evils are growing in power. So you're going to have to move your ass."

Kristoff stifled a chuckle, the words that had just left Athena's lips so out of character and incongruent with her normally serene personality that it was amusing. "Watching too much television again?" he asked, unable to mask a tiny smile.

Athena shrugged. "Not much else to do. Isn't that what humans say when they want someone to take action soon?" She cocked her head and looked at him with an innocent expression.

"Yes," he answered honestly, not wanting to offend her and knowing she was completely cut off from the modern world except for a few electronics. "That's exactly what they'd say." Kristoff didn't add that the words just sounded odd coming from a goddess who was thousands of years old, a deity who had been born an adult with more wisdom and reason than any other creature on Earth. "What did you see?" he asked curiously, wanting to know anything and everything that she had fore-seen for the Sentinels.

She sighed, a long beleaguered exhalation, before replying, "Everything and nothing. You know how frustrating it is when you know change is coming, but not everything is revealed." She leaned regally against the back of her chair and folded her delicate hands on top of the table. "The Evils are growing stronger, more powerful. But the Sentinels will also gain advantages. Be watchful, Kristoff. We can't afford to miss an opportunity. It's important for the Sentinels to gain every edge they possibly can."

Leaning back, Kristoff ran a frustrated hand through his hair, leav-ing some of the blond locks spiked on top of his head. "I've felt it, too. I just don't know exactly *what* is happening." Knowing something was coming, but not knowing exactly what or when it would occur, was exasperating. While his Sentinels thought he was being annoyingly mysterious and evasive, more often than not, he just didn't have spe-cifics until they were revealed to him. Okay...maybe he *did* hide a *few* things, but only information his Sentinels just didn't need to know, or things that would be detrimental for them to find out.

Athena unfolded her hands and laid one of them gently over the fist he held tightly on the table, a gesture of support and comfort. "You will know when it's time for you to know. I just wanted you to be warned and watchful. We've always known the Winston brothers were special. The power will come through them. Soon."

Kristoff had always known those three men were key to the survival of his people. That knowledge had been crystal-clear from the moment he had bargained with them. "But how?" he asked aloud. It was a question he had asked himself many times during the last two centuries, ever since he had converted them from human to Sentinel.

Releasing Kristoff's hand and using her goddess powers, Athena manifested an array of delicacies on the table, and an elaborate tea set. Steam rose from the spout of the teapot as she reached for it. "Let's have tea and share our knowledge. Everything is better with tea."

He nodded automatically, thinking that he'd really rather have a glass of Scotch, or maybe a whole bottle. He might not feel the effects of the alcohol, but the fiery burn caused by the excellent whiskey was much more suited to his present mood than tea.

Like it or not, he was responsible for every Sentinel on the planet, male or female, and the majority of them were more human than demon, and to say that some days he had conflicting emotions about his destiny would be putting it mildly. It was a duty and an honor, a crushing burden and an exhilarating challenge. But mostly…it was just who he was, and he accepted the albatross easily, donned the mantle of king with pride. Because he *was* proud of the Sentinels…most of the time. They had, after all, kept the fight between good and evil in balance since the time of the ancient gods.

Heaving a very masculine sigh, he accepted the dainty cup from Athena, glad he at least had her occasional company to discuss the things that he couldn't share with anyone else. Athena helped center him, and had given him wisdom when he had become a little too hot-headed in his younger years. He'd asked her once why she still remained when all of the other gods had faded from existence. Her reply had been both wistful and pragmatic, telling him that she would remain until she was no longer needed.

As the goddess started talking, telling him about her visions, Kristoff couldn't imagine a time when Athena *wouldn't* be essential to the continued survival of the Sentinels. They spent the next hour in conversation, sharing their ideas and knowledge before he said goodbye, her melancholic face fading as he transported away.

Kristoff left Athena's enormous home with a lot of questions still plaguing his mind, and very few concrete answers. The only thing he knew for certain was that the lives of some of the Sentinels were about to be altered, and he had work to do to ensure that everything turned out the way it was fated. Because sometimes, even if one were on a predetermined course, one could still get lost. The Winston brothers, all three of them, in their own different ways, needed to heal from their past to fulfill their destiny for the future.

As king, he cared for all of the Sentinels, but Zach, Drew, and Hunter were special, more friends than subjects to him, which created a real internal conflict. He couldn't reveal their destiny, but he'd do everything in his power to make sure they fulfilled it.

Kristoff reappeared in Seattle to complete the first of many tasks on his list, determined that, no matter what, he wouldn't fail.

# Chapter One

*e careful what you wish for; it might come true.*

The oxymoronic saying floated through Zachary Winston's head as he sat with his hands under his chin, listening to the satisfying clack of metal against metal as the two end spheres of his Newton's cradle rose and fell. Kinetic energy, velocity, and scientific explanations were far from his mind at the moment. He simply enjoyed watching the symmetry of the movement, the hypnotic action serving to slightly calm the darkness and bleakness of his demonic soul.

If he had wished more carefully two hundred years ago, his twelve-year-old sister, Sophie, might have actually lived after his bargain with the Sentinel demon king. Zach had agreed to become a Sentinel for eternity in return for fabulous wealth, certain that money could get him the help he needed to save his baby sister from dying of smallpox. It didn't. She had died alone in the squalor of a pest house while he was out trying to steal things to make her more comfortable, and making an eternal bargain that hadn't done a damn thing to help her. The deal had come too late; it wasn't what Sophie needed to save her, and Zach had been left completely alone in the world. The only person in the universe who had cared about him had been ripped from his grasp, regardless of the fact that he had become one of the richest men in the world because of his demon bargain. Actually, he still was one of the richest men in the world, although money meant little to him now. Not after two centuries of guilt and remorse had been plaguing him every single day, his soul growing darker every year.

*I should have made a different wish. Sophie was probably still alive when I struck my bargain with Kristoff.*

Zach had made the wrong wish, one that had left him with two hundred years of loneliness, and enough time to curse himself for not thinking harder about Kristoff's offer before agreeing so readily. He would have made a deal with the devil himself to save the sister he had adored, and for whom he had been responsible after the death of his mother.

Zach didn't remember his father. A fisherman, he'd died in a violent storm at sea soon after Sophie was born. His mother had been left in a poor area of London with nothing except two young children to feed and no money. Zach knew his mother had been a prostitute, using the only commodity she had to feed herself and her two children, and he had never condemned her for it. How in the hell else was a woman with two young children going to make money in the early nineteenth century? His mother could have given him and Sophie up, sent them away, but she didn't. Instead, she had become old before her time, developing consumption after years of struggling to take care of them. Before she had breathed her last, she'd made him promise to watch out for his younger sister, and Zach had taken that deathbed promise seriously. Still, he had failed both his mother and his sister. Both of them were dead, his innocent sister Sophie at the tender age of twelve.

*Why wasn't it me who died? It should have been me!*

"Playing with your balls again, I see." The deep, gravelly voice sounded from the doorway of his plush office. His eyes rose as he glanced at Kristoff Agares, the Sentinel demon king, as he swaggered into Zach's office with a smirk, not waiting for an invitation. Not that he ever did. Kristoff answered to no one as far as Zach knew, and he did exactly as he pleased.

Zach reached out a hand and stopped the clacking executive toy, focusing his scowling attention on the tall blond demon. Although he had gained a grudging respect for Kristoff over the last two centuries,

Zach had never quite let go of the fact that the Sentinel demon king hadn't shown up a little earlier, in time to save Sophie instead of him. But he hadn't. Kristoff had intervened when Zach was caught stealing and had made his bargain with him. Later that same day, when Kristoff had come to complete Zach's bargain and transform him into a Sentinel, the demon king had found Zach clawing at Sophie's grave, angry and half crazed because he hadn't even been able to say goodbye, hadn't been there when his sister had perished and been dumped in a mass grave along with other bodies from the pest house. Kristoff had transported him away, taking him into his own home to give him time to get over his grief and anger. Unfortunately, although his anger and grief had lessened over the last two hundred years, his guilt and remorse still remained.

Kristoff lowered his muscular body into the roomy leather chair in front of Zach's desk as he remarked casually, "You need to find your *radiant*. You have absolutely no sense of humor."

"Did it ever occur to you that your stupid comments aren't really all that funny?" Zach muttered as he frowned at Kristoff.

"Nope. I'm hilarious. You're just in desperate need of a *radiant*," Kristoff told him with a grin. "You need to get laid."

*His radiant? Oh, hell no.*

A *radiant* was the Sentinel equivalent of a mate, the one who would bring light back into his dark soul. All Zach had ever found were women who wanted to lighten his damn wallet…not his soul.

*Once…just one time…I'd like to find a woman who wants me and not my money.*

Truth was, Zach had given up on taking women to bed just for sex a long time ago. It just seemed to make him darker, and more restless. The emptiness of casual sexual romps just no longer appealed to him. It left him even more lonely and unsatisfied than he'd been prior to the sexual encounters.

"I don't need my *radiant* to get fucked," Zach grumbled defensively, although he hadn't gotten fucked for quite some time.

"Trust me. You need more than a quick, unemotional screw." Kristoff's expression grew serious, his voice concerned.

"I assume you're here for a reason?" Zach shot his superior a glare, wanting to change the subject. He *did* want more, needed more, but it wasn't something he actually wanted to discuss at the moment. He was too restless, too edgy, and he'd been that way for a while now. It was as though he was just waiting, biding his time until some type of mysterious metamorphosis happened, and the uncomfortable, impatient feeling was making his fuse shorter every damn day.

Kristoff shrugged. "Aren't I always?" He leaned forward and shoved a file across the desk toward Zach. "Your next assignment."

Zach actually released a sigh of relief. It had been a few weeks since he had been given a mission. He needed the distraction, the challenge. Boredom wasn't good for him. It gave him too much time to think, and thinking usually led to regrets and guilt. Honestly, he didn't mind being a Sentinel, and he didn't regret that part of his bargain. There was nothing he loved more than letting Evils give him a reason to annihilate the ugly little bastards.

*Yeah, I need a mission. I have too much time on my hands right now.*

Zach didn't need to worry much about business because there was absolutely no reason why he should. He'd always be wealthy. Winston Industries was worth billions and he knew it always would be. Any decision he made would be the right one to increase his wealth. Being rich was part of the demon bargain he had made two hundred years ago. Demon magic would make it a certainty that he stayed a billionaire, which pretty much took the challenge out of work for him, leaving him with too much time to think, unless he was on assignment.

Zach lifted the file curiously. "A recruitment?"

Kristoff shook his head. "A rescue."

Zach's hand halted before he opened the file, his eyes returning to Kristoff with a startled expression. "The Evils are abducting an innocent? How?" It was a stupid question and he knew it. The bastards had a multitude of trickery and deceit to capture blameless souls. But his surprise over being given a rescue instead of a recruitment disturbed him in a visceral way, an instant denial ringing in his head, telling him that he would suck at rescue. Hadn't he failed in the task of keeping an innocent from harm in the past? *Oh, hell no. Not a rescue.* He was used to recruiting salvageable souls that were straddling the line between good and evil to become Sentinels. He was the last Sentinel that should be left with the care of a blameless soul. More than likely, he'd screw it up; the Evils would take the victim, and he'd end up with another death on his conscience. Whoever the poor unfortunate human might be, that individual deserved a hell of a lot better Sentinel than him as a savior.

Truly evil demons could manipulate humans in any number of ways. Their main goal was to sway as many untainted and unsuspecting humans to the demon realm as possible, using whatever means available. The catch was...the uncorrupt human had to agree, had to give permission to be taken, even when not entirely understanding what the bargain with the Evils entailed, since the assholes weren't exactly into full disclosure. Wallowing in the pain caused by corruption of an unblemished soul was empowerment to an Evil. The purer the soul, the more power the Evil absorbed. And once the vow to go with the Evils was uttered, that was one more soul lost to the Sentinels. And if there was anything a Sentinel really hated, it was to be defeated by an Evil. The instinct to win was strong, the trait imbedded since the creation of the Sentinels and passed on by demon magic whenever a new recruit was changed and indoctrinated.

Kristoff nodded his head to the file that Zach was holding as he replied, "Emotional manipulation. Not uncommon for the Evils, but pretty dirty this time."

Zach opened the folder. His breath *whooshed* out of his lungs as his inspection was met with the blinding smile of a veritable angel. With flame-colored hair that tumbled over her shoulders, Katrina "Kat" Larson-the name on the file label-was definitely an unholy temptation. Zach viewed all of her pictures slowly, taking in the creamy light skin and curvy, generous figure in every photo. Every picture showed her laughing or smiling and her spirit was almost infectious, even via the glossy images.

*No wonder the Evils want her. Her sweetness practically jumps out of the photos.*

Kristoff spoke as Zach continued to stare at the woman's pictures. "Twenty-seven-year-old female. Coerced to sacrifice herself to the Evils for a week in exchange for her eight-year-old nephew's life...her twin sister's child. He suffers from leukemia, which is currently in remission. They apparently told her he wouldn't die if she would come with them to the demon realm for a week."

"And will it save him?" Zach asked distractedly as he placed his hand over the smiling face of the woman to absorb her information, rather than wait for it to be revealed on paper. He couldn't read her thoughts unless he was actually close to her, but he could get the general facts faster by absorbing the written words in the file.

Kristoff leaned forward as his voice lowered. "No demon has power over life and death from disease, Zach. Not even me. We can see the outcome sometimes, but we can't interfere. I've told you that. You just choose not to accept it. The Evils can only damage souls or kill a human victim who agreed to bargain. They don't have the power to cure an incurable disease." Kristoff sighed as he leaned his muscular body back into the soft leather of the chair. "They told her that her nephew would live...which is true. What they didn't tell her is that it has nothing to do with any power *they* have. Her nephew's disease will stay in remission whether she goes to the demon realm or not. They've managed to use her fear for her nephew's life to manipulate her without actually lying."

"Bastards! So they led her to believe her nephew would die unless she struck the bargain and went with them?" Zach snarled as he closed the file, his brown eyes starting to glow amber as he looked at Kristoff, his face revealing his frustration and anger. Shit...he hated those ugly little bastards. He'd seen humans who they'd manipulated and taken to the demon realm, souls the Sentinels hadn't been able to save. Sometimes they killed their human victims in the demon realm after absorbing all the power they could get from the individual. Occasionally, they sent the bodies back alive, but drained of their souls, completely lifeless. That particular action was usually done as a taunt to the Sentinels, and it generally worked. His kind had a very hard time not being angry when confronted with the harm done to a human who couldn't be saved.

"Obviously they didn't say that directly," Kristoff answered unhappily. "They just told her that her nephew would live if she gave up a week of her life to live in the demon realm. Not exactly a lie, but definitely an extreme evasion of the truth."

"Dammit. She'll be destroyed, a shell of who she was before leaving… if they even send her back alive. All for nothing." Zach's hands clenched into fists, his knuckles whitening with the pressure. The thought of the smiling, innocent, vivacious redhead being turned into an empty body with none of her spirit left made his guts roll, although he wasn't quite sure why. It wasn't as if he didn't see it happen frequently, but his emotional reaction to this particular case unsettled him. Maybe it was because he didn't normally take these types of assignments.

"Not if you get to her first." Kristoff's eyes were intense as he nailed Zach with an urgent look. "She doesn't understand that they mean to steal the life from her soul and she hasn't given consent. You need to convince her, Zach. She has a soul worth saving." He hesitated before adding, "She's…special." Kristoff sounded like he wanted to add more, but simply shook his head.

"Why me? I'm a recruiter…not a rescuer. Why didn't you give the job to Drew or Hunter?" Drew and Hunter were rescuing Sentinels. Zach… wasn't, and he didn't want to be, although he was reluctant to give this particular assignment to another after seeing the victim and absorbing her general history. Something about her intrigued him, made him want to learn more about her, see her in person.

Zach recruited new Sentinels, humans who had nowhere to go, no one to help them…and who were ready to leap from good to evil because of their circumstances. He offered them the same bargain Kristoff had offered Zach a few centuries ago. *That* was Zach's designation, a demon duty completely different from that of his two partners in Winston Industries. Zach, Drew, and Hunter posed as brothers, all leading Winston Industries together, but they weren't actually blood-related. They had just all wished for the same damn thing, had wanted the same demon bargain. *Money.* And they had gotten it. Drew was the only one of the trio who seemed to be happy with his bargain. Zach was still filled with regret, even after two centuries. And Hunter was downright bitter and angry.

*Be careful what you wish for…*

"Drew is busy with another mission, Hunter is...unavailable, and I have another urgent situation. It has to be you, or Kat will probably end up in the demon realm," Kristoff replied, his voice neutral, but his eyes were intense as he stared Zach down, forcing him to make a decision.

"How long do I have?" Zach replied, focused on his mission, determined that he wouldn't screw up this time. There was no way the Evils were going to get their claws into *this* one. The woman looked sweet, innocent. Just the thought of her soul being drained of goodness had him half crazed.

*No wonder I'm a damn recruiter. How the hell do Drew and Hunter tolerate doing this type of assignment day after day?*

"Sundown. They'll appear for her final consent and take her," Kristoff replied without hesitation.

Zach stared at the large glass windows that lined one wall of his office, overlooking the city. As he saw the late afternoon light beginning to fade, he quirked a dark brow at his boss. "Cutting this a little close... don't you think?"

"Not my fault. I didn't discover the situation until this afternoon." As both men stood and Zach stepped out from behind his desk, Kristoff slapped him hard on the back. "It's nothing you're not capable of, Zach."

Zach scowled as he answered, "I may have to bend a few rules if I can't convince her quickly. You didn't exactly give me enough time to do much persuading."

A smile curved Kristoff's lips as he answered noncommittally, "I think you know how to bend the rules without completely breaking them like Hunter does."

Zach didn't reply. With a curt nod to Kristoff, he allowed himself to fade out until he disappeared completely.

Kristoff's expression turned to one of satisfaction as he watched Zach's form completely disappear before shimmering out of view himself, leaving the plush, high-rise office completely abandoned.

# Chapter Two

*lmost sunset. Almost sunset.*

Kat Larson shivered as she dropped her suitcase near the door of her tiny, shabby apartment, trying to reassure herself for about the millionth time that she was doing the right thing. It was only a week. She'd give herself up forever to the flames of Hell if it meant that Stevie would survive.

She cringed as a sharp knock sounded on her door. Heart racing and hands shaking, she reached for the knob. *Since when do demons knock politely at my door?*

They had started showing up in her nightmares and had progressed to appearing before her whenever and wherever they damn well pleased, battering at her emotions with scenarios about what could happen to Stevie in the future. In the end, she had been ready to agree to almost anything to make them stop, unable to bear the imagery of how her precious nephew could suffer in the future if she didn't agree to the demons' demands.

Wiping her sweaty palms on her jeans, she took a deep breath and pulled open the door.

Kat's face registered her surprise at seeing the man who stood in front of her. She recognized him. Not that she exactly mingled with people of Zachary Winston's caliber, but she had seen his handsome picture on the wall of the sleek high-rise building, the headquarters of his corporation. Several times a week. She had a plant and flower maintenance business and Winston Industries was her biggest client.

She'd seen the pictures of all three Winston brothers side-by-side, but it was *this* man who drew her gaze to his picture more often than it should.

*It's his eyes. He looks sad…and haunted.*

All three brothers had dark hair and eyes, but that was where the resemblance ended. Drew Winston's eyes were mischievous, Hunter Winston's angry, but Zachary Winston's gaze reflected some sort of sorrow, and something about his image had always moved her, making her wonder what was in his past that made sadness linger in such gorgeous eyes.

It was hard not to give Zachary Winston a second look…or a third. Oh hell, the tall muscular body, currently covered by an expensive charcoal-gray suit, was difficult to ignore. Combined with his gorgeous face, dark brown eyes, and neatly trimmed raven-black hair, the guy was every woman's fantasy. In person, he carried an aura of danger and masculinity that sent her heart into overdrive.

What the heck was *he* doing *here?*

"Mr. Winston," she acknowledged him politely, her voice a little breathless. "What are you doing here?" Was it about the job she was doing? *Oh God, please don't let him be here to fire my company.* Kat desperately needed that income.

Had she taken a rational moment to think about the possibility whether Zachary Winston, billionaire extraordinaire, would come to her low-income apartment building just to fire her in person, Kat would have laughed at her own stupidity. Like Zachary Winston even knew who she was, or that she was on his radar? But Kat wasn't exactly reasoning well at that moment. She was still busy freaking out over the fact that she was about to make a bargain with a couple of ugly little demons.

"Ms. Larson." He nodded, giving her a perplexed look. "Have we met?"

"No, sir. My company does the plant maintenance for your building. I've seen your picture." Kat continued to gape at him as she continued.

"Is this about business? I thought I was doing a good job." She cursed her shaky voice as she questioned him. Could this day get any worse?

*I'm going to end up both making a demon bargain and losing my biggest client in the same day?*

His lips turned up as his eyes raked over her in an intrusive, assessing manner. He didn't even try to hide his perusal of her body as he answered, "Not corporation business, Katrina. I believe you were expecting someone to be here."

*Oh. My. God. Please tell me Zachary Winston is NOT a demon. I practically drool over his photo every time I see it. Please don't tell me I've been salivating over a damn demon.*

He was someone she respected as her client and he wasn't even a tiny bit similar to the disgusting trolls that usually tormented her. Before she could think about it, she blurted out, "You're a demon, here to take me away?"

He answered carefully, "I am indeed a demon here to take you. Are you coming with me willingly?"

*Shit. Shit. Shit.*

Kat saw every naughty fantasy she'd ever had about Zachary Winston fly out the window as he stared intensely at her, the question hanging ominously in the air.

"Yes." She could barely get the reply out of her mouth as her throat tightened with fear. What choice did she really have? If she wanted her nephew to live, there was really nothing else to say, no other way to respond.

"Then come." He held his hand out to her. "We have a bargain to make."

His voice was kind, yet firm, and she shivered as she prepared to leave her apartment. She lifted her suitcase and pulled the door closed. Her hands trembled as she tried to lock it, her mind whirling with confusion, still stunned that a man whose image she had admired from afar was actually a demon in disguise.

Zach took the keys calmly from her hand and dropped them casually into his pocket. She heard the deadbolt engage without him even touching the lock.

*Crap.* This was starting to *really* freak her out. Not that the previous demons hadn't had her wondering if her sanity was slipping away from her...but Zachary Winston? The man looked a hell of a lot more like a wet dream than a nightmare.

Zach grinned as he held his hand out again and as she went to take it nervously, the hallway suddenly filled with a sense of danger that sent a chill down her spine and temporarily paralyzed her body, causing her to drop the suitcase to the floor. It was a reaction she had experienced before, and it was completely unnerving, her mind panicking as her body stayed incapacitated.

The two evil creatures she had dealt with previously appeared at her side.

Them...she recognized!

Kat had no idea what their real names were, or if they even had any, but she called them Dwarf and Goblin in her mind. Both of them were repulsive and they radiated an evil that made her break out in a cold sweat. They were actually both fairly small with spiky black hair, but what they lacked in height, they made up for in strength and malice. With gleaming red eyes and sunken features, they would never be mistaken for a human or anything else except for what they were-evil demons.

Dwarf pulled her hand roughly to her side, twisting her wrist as he held it against her hip. "You are already promised to us." Dwarf barely reached her shoulder in height, but for such a small man-or maybe she should say a small demon?-his grip was like iron. Kat flinched at the tight hold that could easily snap her bones.

Zach stepped forward, grabbing the clawed fist Dwarf was using to confine her arm, removing it from Kat's wrist. "If she had given her final agreement to a bargain...you would already be gone," he informed them in a low, growling voice as he twisted the offender's wrist until the bone cracked, before releasing it.

The small demon let out a howl that sent a chill down Kat's spine and cradled its arm against his chest as Goblin stepped forward. "She will agree. She was waiting for us."

*Run, Kat. Run.*

Kat's instinct was to flee as her mind commanded. Confusion clouded her brain and she tried desperately to understand what was happening. She couldn't escape. Not only was she being held inert by some sort of supernatural power, but Stevie's life was at stake. If only she understood Zachary Winston's motives, why he was here.

*They're lying. They have no power over your nephew's disease. They're trying to coerce you into the demon realm to destroy your soul. Come with me. Don't let them take you.*

Zachary Winston's urgent baritone drifted into her mind softly, but as she met his eyes…they were glowing more amber than brown. It was a rather eerie feature in an otherwise gorgeous face. His powerful gaze beckoned her and she hesitated for just a moment in indecision.

*Two disgusting little demons that reek of corruption and bad intentions…or Zachary Winston?*

She already knew Dwarf and Goblin were pure evil. She had no idea what to make of Zachary Winston. Was one demon different from another?

*Yes. I'm here to help you. They're here to destroy you.*

She wanted to believe Zachary Winston's matter-of-fact answer that she heard only in her mind, the soothing, deep baritone strangely comforting as it flowed through her head.

Goblin grunted, "Give us your agreement. Now." His voice was demanding, but he didn't touch her. He kept shooting side glances at his buddy, Dwarf. Fear of retaliation from Zachary Winston probably kept the evil demon from roughing her up.

*Promise me something…anything…so that I can take you out of here. There has to be a demon bargain to put you under our protection and take you away. Believe me…these bastards will do nothing but hurt you.*

Kat's eyes darted back and forth between the rich, handsome executive and the irate demons, knowing that she needed to make a choice. Really, the choice shouldn't be all that difficult. But these two vile demons had been particularly prominent in her nightmares, showing her horrible scenarios of what could happen to her nephew.

Goblin loomed closer and she could smell the rancid odor of his body. "Do it now, bitch. Come with us or you know what could happen."

She shot a terrified look at Zachary, afraid that if she made the wrong choice it could cost her nephew his life.

*They can do nothing to interfere with your nephew's disease. Come with me now. I can protect you. Promise me something. Anything. Make a demon's bargain with me so I can get you the hell out of here. I'd love to dust both of these little bastards, but I can't unless they give me a reason.*

She looked from Goblin to Zachary...and her decision was made, half gut instinct, half common sense. Goblin was completely dark; Zachary's intentions were still a mystery.

Kat would rather take her chances with the unknown than with the malodorous, evil demons that were certain to cause her harm. At least with Zachary Winston, there was a possibility of survival. If she had to believe either one or the other, instinct was telling her to go with Zachary.

*A demon's bargain?* What did you promise a demon? Zachary Winston didn't need money and she didn't have any to give him anyway.

*Promise to do anything I want for a week. Give me the same time bargain as you made with them. Spend one week with me.*

Kat jerked visibly as his suggestion sounded loud and clear in her mind. Was he joking? Why would he want her for a week? It made no sense.

*Just do it.*

Zachary's tone was demanding. As Goblin got bolder and started crowding her, she panicked. "Yes. Yes. I'll do it. I'll go with you for a week and do anything you want." Her voice was trembling but audible as the statement flew out of her mouth on the wings of anxiety.

"Done." Zach spoke aloud immediately after her agreement, grabbing her hand.

Kat's head swam as Zach pulled her into his hard, solid body and everything faded to black.

# Chapter Three

"What the fuck have I done?" Zach murmured aloud as he observed the fiery-haired woman still resting unconscious on his black silk sheets. He had to clench his fingers, digging his nails into his palms to resist the urge to sit on the side of the bed and bury his hands in that long, curly hair to feel its silky texture. Just seeing the contrast of the color against the black sheets and imagining the curls of the same shade between her thighs was making his cock as hard as diamonds.

*She belongs to me.*

Zach had known almost immediately that Kat was his *radiant,* and every possessive male instinct in his body had sprung to life, emotions he had never even known he could feel. A spark of light had ignited in his shadowy soul the moment she had opened the door. Kat was capable of lightening his soul, relieving the darkness of his demon existence. It would be ecstasy for him after two hundred years of darkness, but it would mean a sacrifice for her. Who wanted to spend eternity with a demon? Unfortunately, it didn't stop him from wanting her more than he'd ever wanted anything in his entire existence.

Kat moaned as she started to awaken and his cock ached for release from the jeans that he had changed into after his hasty transport home. In his eagerness to remove her from danger, he had teleported them too quickly, faster than her human body could manage without falling into the black abyss of unconsciousness to protect itself from harm.

He gave up his internal battle and seated himself on the bed, waiting anxiously to see her jade-green eyes open. Her eyelids fluttered before she looked up at him, dazed and disoriented.

"Where am I?" she asked hesitantly, her voice husky and confused. Zach watched Kat slowly focus, her gaze flitting nervously around the room, finally landing on his face. "Mr. Winston? Oh, God, I was hoping that what I remembered was a nightmare," she finished with a small groan as she sat up, rubbing her face with her palm.

A rueful smile formed on his face as he wondered if he should be offended at being remembered as part of a nightmare. *Damn. I thought I was a wet dream.* He had liked *that* errant thought when he had heard it in her mind. "It was real, Kat. You're at my home and you need to remain here until the week we bargained for is over. You'll then be completely under our protection."

*I'll go with you for a week and do anything you want.*

Her agreement fluttered through his mind and Zach's gut clenched. What the hell had prompted him to suggest that asinine bargain? He could have accepted anything...but he knew the suggestion had popped forward because it was his soul and his body's greatest desire. He'd been a selfish bastard, a demon demanding his *radiant*, and now they would both pay for his stupidity. He found her so incredibly attractive that he knew he'd end up spending the whole week in a constant state of arousal. What he wanted was her beneath him, moaning his name as he claimed her. In fact, he was fucking obsessed by the thought.

Kat, being under the influence of a demon's bargain, would feel compelled to satisfy anything he wanted-to the point of pain if she didn't heed the compulsion. Demon bargains were *very literal*. He'd have to block his wants and his compulsions from her, which would be pretty damn difficult because, at the moment, his demon instincts were clamoring loudly for the voluptuous woman in his bed.

Zach couldn't leave Kat unprotected. He had already tried to contact Kristoff, but the Sentinel demon king had claimed that Zach needed to complete the bargain he had made so that Kat could remain under their protection. Kristoff had replied with a hint of laughter in his voice. *The asshole.* Somehow, Kristoff knew this was going to be torture for Zach. *And the twisted bastard is enjoying the fact that I'm uncomfortable.*

Kat's face fell as she looked at him in horror. "The bargain. Was that for real?"

Zach shifted uncomfortably as he answered in a husky voice, "Yes."

"Why? Why would you suggest that?" Kat looked at him anxiously, her face flushing.

Zach shrugged as his eyes met her startled expression. "I guess I suggested it without really thinking." His hand reached out with a will of its own to thread through her auburn mass of curls. He nearly groaned at the silky softness. "I may be your rescuer…but I'm still a demon."

Zach admitted to himself that the dark, wicked side of him had wanted her locked into the bargain. She was so beautiful to him that he hadn't been able to resist. He hadn't wanted to resist. The man in him knew it was unfair and struggled with the ethics of his actions, but his demon side was screaming to possess her and didn't give a damn how he got her. He'd never really had a major struggle between the demon he was and the humanity he'd developed, but he had a bad feeling both were about to go to war…big time.

Kat rubbed her palms against the worn denim of her jeans before crossing her arms over her ample breasts. "No offense, but I think you are way past due for an eye exam, Mr. Winston. I'm a plain, overly curvy redhead with very few physically attractive features. Not exactly a woman who would make any man feel consumed with lust. I think we're pretty safe."

"You're the most tempting woman I've ever met. I'll keep you from any physical harm, but you're far from safe with me, Kat." His voice was low and tortured, as though he couldn't stop the flow of words from his mouth. He pulled his hand from her hair reluctantly as he finished, "Call me Zach." Mr. Winston applied to all of his brothers, and Zach craved intimacy with Kat desperately. He wanted her to know exactly who she was with at all times.

Zach stared at Kat's ripe, full lips as her tongue darted out to moisten them, his mind wandering to carnal ideas of where he'd like to have those lips and that tongue right now. His internal struggle prompted him to move away, but she reached for him as he was about to rise. Her arms snaked around his neck and she drew his mouth toward hers before he could move. As her warm, welcoming lips met his, satisfying one of his many longings that were associated with this woman… moving wasn't even a consideration. His desires were flowing into her mind, and she was consumed by the need to do anything he wanted.

*I need her. Just one kiss. One intimate act to pacify my desire to possess her.*

All thoughts of humanity fled as their lips met, and his darker instincts took control.

Kat groaned as she slid her tongue into Zach's willing warm mouth, shivering at the intensity of their hot, passionate embrace. He rolled on the bed, sprawling his naked torso on top of hers as his arms wrapped around her in a powerful hold.

Her hands explored his shirtless muscled back and chest, unable to get enough of his heated naked skin as he took control. He nibbled and nipped at her bottom lip, and then teased it with his tongue before devouring her mouth again…and again.

Kat was breathless, whimpering into his mouth as she squirmed beneath him, her body and mind not accustomed to being devoured with this sort of passion. *He wants me, really desires me.* She could feel his hard shaft pressing against the confines of his jeans, engorged and begging for release.

She ground up against him, needing to satiate his body. She could see crystal-clear flashes of scenarios in her mind.

*Her…*on her knees, sucking him to completion.

*Him…*his mouth between her thighs, licking her into a state of complete ecstasy.

*Both of them…*straining together as his cock slammed into her over and over again, their bodies meeting in an all-consuming frenzy.

Kat broke her mouth away from his to pant, "Please, Zach." *What did he want? Any of them? All of them?* "Let me satisfy you. You want it. I want it."

Her whole body was on fire with need-his needs, his visions-yet her senses were responding with a desire just as strong, just as devastating.

"Shit," he cursed as he wrenched away from her. He shot off the bed and stood beside it, panting as if he had run a marathon. "I'm sorry, Kat. You're feeling my wants. It's the damn bargain."

His eyes were glowing amber, throwing flickering sparks in the darkening room that reminded her of fireflies lighting up a dark night.

Without another word, he strode to the bathroom and closed the door.

Kat felt her eyes mist with tears, her urge to follow him almost irresistible. What in the hell was happening to her? Two separate sets of needs were bombarding her, both with the same goal. She felt the compulsion to fulfill his sexual urges, but that passionate interlude on the bed had conjured a few of her own. How could it not? Zach was so hot that she could almost climax just from looking at him, feeling the testosterone that hummed through his body and into the air around them as he was devouring her. Having him come on to her with that much passion was overwhelming, and his withdrawal had left her cold and empty. She knew it was just an illusion, but for that short period of time, she had felt-complete.

*It was just a kiss. It didn't mean anything.*

Sitting up, she wrapped her arms around herself, shivering with emotion. A month ago, she had been just an average twenty-seven-year old woman, struggling to survive in a world where there wasn't much opportunity for a college dropout. She had left college after only a year when her sister Nora had given birth to Stevie. He'd been unwanted by his father, and she and her sister had worked together to take care of him. Kat had started her business caring for plants to accommodate her sister's hours as a secretary. Daycare was expensive and Kat was able to switch her jobs around to care for Stevie when Nora was working.

Their parents had both died in a car accident only days before Kat and Nora had graduated from high school, leaving the twins very little to survive on. Nora had been all she had. When Stevie came along, Kat had thrown herself into the task of helping them all survive until very recently.

Nora had married three months ago, luckily to a man who loved both her and Stevie. Kat had been happy when her twin had finally settled and found her happiness…but now, part of her felt lost. She still saw her nephew and sister often, but they didn't need her anymore, weren't part of her life every day, and Kat now realized how much her whole world had revolved around them.

Sometimes she felt so incredibly alone. For so many years, she hadn't had time to think about relationships, Nora and Stevie being her primary concern and companionship. Caring for her nephew had been demanding because he had been a sick little boy and there hadn't been time to think about what she wanted for herself. She didn't regret one moment of those years. Kat loved her sister and Stevie with all of her heart, but now that they didn't live with her anymore and weren't constantly around…she wasn't quite sure where she belonged or what she wanted to do. She was basically drifting, her whole purpose in life ripped away from her, leaving her suddenly bereft for the first time in her adult life. The madness, the endless cycle of work and fighting for Stevie's survival were suddenly gone, leaving her wandering and restless.

She had to go back to college. Kat had decided that almost immediately, but saving up the money was a challenge.

There was no special man in her life. There never had been except for one boyfriend in college who had dumped her quickly when she had dropped out to help take care of her sister and her nephew. Still in his college partying mode, he wasn't the type of guy who wanted a girlfriend with a boatload of adult responsibility.

Kat's full-figured body with its voluptuous ass and abundant curves wasn't exactly a man magnet. Add her girl-next-door face and her bright copper hair…and you had a woman who never got a first glance, much less a second. She and Nora were fraternal twins, and somehow her beautiful, svelte, auburn-haired sibling had gotten the gorgeous genes. Kat had always joked the she had gotten whatever was left over. Truthfully, she wasn't hideous, but she was honest with herself.

*But I sensed Zach's desire for me. He really wanted me.* The reasons for *that* she just couldn't fathom. He was rich, gorgeous as sin, and probably the sexiest man she had ever seen. Or was he a demon? All she knew was he had felt very male, very hot, and utterly decadent.

Kat sighed as she heard the water shut off in the bathroom, wondering why her body still ached for him. The tension was leaving her body, leaving behind only a dull longing. Either Zach was closing his thoughts or the demon was satisfied.

*Demons.* Kat shook her head and tightened her arms around her body, still shocked that they truly existed. The nightmares she had been able to discount as just an overactive imagination. When the horrid little creatures had started showing up in the flesh…she could no longer deny that they did indeed exist…and they were stalking her. Hell, before her personal experience, she had believed that demons only existed in spirit, wanting to possess a human body.

Her breath hitched as Zach came out of the bathroom, the illumination from the open door bathing the whole bedroom with light. He was dressed in a fresh pair of jeans and a t-shirt. His hair was damp and his eyes had turned back to a sexy chocolate brown. Her core flooded just from looking at him. Thank God he had covered that tempting torso and chest with fabric.

Except…she already knew what lay beneath the light cotton: an incredibly built male body that her fingers itched to touch again.

"I do want to possess you." His harsh voice was deep as he skewered her with an intense look, his eyes roaming over her with a possessive expression, his demeanor tortured.

"What?" Kat answered, confused.

"I'm a demon in human form." He stalked her slowly, moving toward the bed. "I'm not a spirit, and yes, I have darkness in my soul." Reaching the bed, he bent down slowly, his mouth whispering against her ear in a low, growling voice. "And right now I'm a demon that wants to take over a body, but the only body I want to possess is yours. I want to be inside you, not to torment you, but to satisfy you until you can think of nothing but me." He straightened in a slow lazy stretch, his muscular biceps flexing as he came back up to his full, impressive height.

Kat shivered, the warmth of his breath and his erotic words still tingling against her ear. *Oh. Shit.* Men just didn't look at her this way, react to her this way. And her body was on hormone overload, as though every feminine part of her was reacting to some mysterious male pheromone he was emitting from that incredibly masculine form.

*Shake it off, Kat. This guy is way out of your league. Not to mention the fact that he's a demon.* She tried to muster her common sense, but it wasn't easy when her brain was scrambled from looking at the hottest male she'd ever seen. And his suggestive comments were really messing with her head.

"Is what you said true? Will my nephew really be okay?" Her voice was breathless. She turned her eyes toward the wall. Maybe if she didn't look at him, she wouldn't feel the driving need to touch him, an instinct that was nearly overwhelming her.

"He will. He would have stayed in remission whether you had gone with the Evils or not." Zach slid his large body into a chair in the corner of the room, his elbows resting on his knees. Kat could feel his warm gaze and she couldn't resist a peek at him.

His look was fierce, but not malicious like the previous dark demons she had dealt with in the flesh and in her nightmares. She asked him hesitantly, "If the demons we encountered were evil…what does that make you?"

"I'm a demon, Kat. A Sentinel. We try to save souls and we recruit others, those who are living without much hope, to become Sentinels if their soul is still intact. We were created by the gods eons ago to help keep the evil demons in check." He diverted his eyes as he continued. "It doesn't make me good. I'm still a demon and my soul is still dark. It just makes me a better alternative than the Evils. They would have sent you back to the human realm as a shell, your soul completely destroyed. Or they would have killed you after they had tortured you to increase their power. They feed off human souls."

Kat felt a shiver down her spine as she realized how close she had come to making a decision that would have destroyed her without any benefit to her nephew. What would have become of her if Zach hadn't showed up? He made her feel safe, even if he was a demon. "I think you're better than you think you are."

"If you could see the thoughts I'm having about you right now you wouldn't think so," he grumbled back. "It's going to be a long week."

Kat's heart accelerated and her palms were damp. Why would Zach have those kinds of thoughts…about her? He could have almost any woman he wanted.

"Don't want another woman. I want you. I think you're the most beautiful woman I've ever seen, in every way," he answered immediately.

*Damn. I wish he'd quit saying those things.* It made her feel awkward and confused.

She looked at him suspiciously. She hadn't spoken aloud. "You're reading my thoughts again." Just as he had outside her apartment.

"Yes."

"Well…stop it. It's intrusive and it makes me uncomfortable," she scolded him lightly.

He grinned as he leaned back in the chair. "But it's so much more interesting that way. I like to get your thoughts completely uncensored."

She stood up and put her hands on her hips. "If you have a question, feel free to ask, but get out of my head."

Zach rose from his chair slowly, still smiling at her fierce expression and defensive stance. "I'll try to block them," he told her in a voice that sorely lacked conviction.

His curving lips were slightly wicked and a lock of his dark wayward hair fell over his forehead in such a haphazard sexy manner that just looking at him had her heart thundering. The man really *was* a demon. Kat didn't quite believe he would totally block her out. His look told her that he would do as he pleased, whenever he pleased.

"Kat…if that were true, we'd be rolling around in that bed naked right now." His voice was seductive and low, a bedroom-voice that made Kat think about black silk sheets and have visions of the two of them naked and abandoned on top of them, Zach taking her until she was crying out his name in total ecstasy.

"You just relieved yourself. In the shower. I could sense it. You were satisfied," she blurted out before she could censor herself. Not that guarding her words would actually help. Zach seemed pretty adept at reading every one of her thoughts.

"Yep. All I had to do was think about the same scene you were just imagining and it didn't take long," he admitted shamelessly.

Kat nearly groaned. He had stroked himself to images of fucking her. "I-I-you did?"

"I did. And I'm far from satisfied. It barely took the edge off. I'm still aching to be inside you," he informed her bluntly.

So much for getting him to stop talking about sex by reminding him that he had just gotten relief. He seemed to blatantly enjoy the fact that she had sensed his release and had no shame in admitting it or turning her face bright pink with his words. The man was completely shameless.

He shot her a devilish look as she blushed, but he changed the subject. "What would you like for dinner?"

In her present state of arousal…even *that* sounded like a provocative question. As she glanced at his mischievous expression, she decided that it was meant to be. "I'm not picky, as you can probably tell. I devour just about anything."

His brows shot up and he laughed at her with his eyes, shooting her a glance that said he would like to be her next meal.

"You are totally depraved," she accused him with a laugh. She couldn't help herself. He was teasing her mercilessly, but it was intoxicating to have a man like Zach flirt with her so outrageously. It was actually a new experience that both thrilled and unsettled her, making her almost believe he really desired *her*.

His face changed instantly, his expression intense and dangerous. "I do desire you, Kat. More than you can imagine."

*Damn.* She couldn't have a single thought that he wouldn't hear. The air became electric and she shifted uncomfortably. Maybe if she tried to shield her thoughts, he wouldn't pick them up.

"It won't work. I have to block you." He motioned her toward the open bedroom door.

"Well…do it. I hate someone creeping around in my brain," she told him indignantly as she exited the bedroom and waited for him to lead the way to the kitchen.

"I'll try," he told her solemnly, but his eyes were shining with sinful amusement.

As he passed her, she couldn't help admiring his broad shoulders and an ass that would make a nun take a second look.

She thought she heard a snicker.

"Zach." Her voice held a warning.

He held up a hand. "I'm trying, I'm trying."

She didn't think he was really trying much at all, but she didn't say anything else. He *had* rescued her from a horrible fate. Maybe there was only so much he was capable of controlling.

He was, after all, a demon.

She followed him, leaving enough distance to continue to admire his swaggering backside, unable to tear her eyes away.

He was right…it *was* going to be a very long week.

# Chapter Four

"Why do you think you're not beautiful?" Zach asked as he placed his fork on the empty plate in front of him, thanking the gods that Kat had cooked. Conjuring items that were edible wasn't really easy for a Sentinel, and he couldn't cook worth a shit. He usually ate out with Drew and Hunter, or grabbed food wherever it was convenient. Usually his cupboards were pretty bare, but Kat had managed to make something delicious out of nothing, raiding his canned goods and non-perishable items for a pasta dish.

Kat looked at Zach and rolled her eyes as she stood, gathering their empty plates as she answered, "You really do have lousy eyesight. Is that a demon trait?"

"Nope. Our vision is excellent, even in the dark." He smirked and nodded at the dishes she was holding before adding, "You don't have to do that."

Kat flinched as the plates disappeared from her hands on the way to the sink. "Shit. What was that?" She turned to Zach, frowning.

He slumped in his chair and crossed his arms in front of him. "We might not be able to cook, but we're pretty good at cleaning up messes. We've been doing it for a very long time."

Kat turned completely toward Zach, looking around the kitchen, taking in the fact that it was once again spotless. "Everything's done?"

she asked, her voice incredulous. "Wow. That's even better than having a dishwasher." She looked at him in awe.

The irony of the fact that she was looking at him like *that,* simply because he could make a dirty kitchen suddenly clean, didn't escape him. Although he loved the expression of admiration on her face directed toward him, he'd much rather see it because he had done something to earn it. Then again, maybe in her mind, he had. Zach could see Kat's memories, and he unashamedly flashed back to Kat, exhausted, but still working to keep up with domestic chores and caring for her sick nephew after she'd put in a long day or evening of work. And she'd done it all quite happily, with no regrets, because she loved her nephew and sister.

*How can she not know how fucking attractive she is, how damn tempting? Her soul warms mine. She belongs to me.*

Zach stood, his eyes raking over Kat as she stared at him with her intelligent green eyes, his demon urges pounding at him to take her. She was his *radiant*, and for the first time during all the years of his demon existence, he felt warm and alive, the darkness inside him kept at bay by Kat.

*She's mine, dammit.*

Unable to stop himself, he moved closer, backing her up against the refrigerator. He knew his eyes were glowing amber, but she didn't look afraid. She looked…fascinated and mesmerized. "Do you want to know what I see?" he growled, slapping a hand on each side of her body, clenching his jaw as he fought the urge to claim her, trying to block his thoughts so she didn't feel obliged to obey his compulsions.

Kat shook her head slightly at first and then nodded, the muscles in her throat flexing as she swallowed, as though she were unable to speak.

"I see a woman with hair like wild flames that I'd happily allow to incinerate me, and eyes so green and deep that I'd gladly jump into them and drown. She has a body made for wicked, carnal nights and a heart as big as the universe," he told her in a low, husky tone. Unable to stop himself, he buried a hand in her silky tresses and brought his mouth down to nip her earlobe as he finished, "And best of all, I see a woman who's completely mine."

Zach took a deep breath, his whole body stiffening as he inhaled the fragrance of *her*-his mate, his *radiant*-the irresistible scent making his already erect member strain against the metal buttons of his jeans.

*Fuck. I can't do this. She's under a demon bargain, controlled by compulsion. She doesn't need a demon mate. She deserves better after spending all of her adult life taking care of others. I'm being a selfish bastard.*

His hand fisted in her hair, struggling to contain the urge to unblock his thoughts and let her feel the compulsions.

Dammit. He needed to fight the cravings, the soul-deep longing that had every muscle in his body quivering from trying to leash his demon desires.

*Dominate.*

*Conquer.*

*Take.*

*Mine.*

Zach's actions and thoughts were becoming completely visceral and beyond possessive, his humanity slipping beneath his demon yearning to have his *radiant*.

"Zach," Kat whispered, her arms coming around his neck, urging his mouth to hers.

He felt the warm whisper of her ragged breath against his lips before he completely lost it.

Kat melted into Zach's heated, muscular body as his mouth claimed hers with a dominance that stole her breath and left her gasping against his lips. His velvet tongue demanded her surrender, and she gave it to him while he plundered her mouth as though he were starving...for her.

Her core flooded with molten heat as she thrust her tongue against his, needing to get closer to him, her body and mind demanding it. Her being was deluged with the desire to sate him, the need so strong that her legs went weak from longing. She knew some of the needs belonged to him-his desire, his wants-but an equal amount were completely her own, her senses unable to resist the temptation that was uniquely Zach. Never had a man moved her so much. There was nothing spectacular about her, in looks or personality, yet Zach wanted her; the proof of his desire was pounding in her mind, and against her stomach. And she wanted him almost to the point of insanity, as if her soul were reaching for him, clawing to be joined with him. It was animalistic and primal, and Kat was helpless, intoxicated by her intense desire to be possessed by Zach.

*You're mine, Kat. I need you.* She heard his tormented voice inside her mind as one hot, fiery kiss melted into the next, and his hands cupped her ass, pulling her up and against his rock hard cock, her pussy clenching with the need to have him inside her.

"What the fuck are you doing, Zach?" The booming voice exploded, vibrating through the entire kitchen as Zach's mouth left Kat's and he was yanked away from her, leaving her confused and breathless. She was panting as her hand grasped the handle of the refrigerator to keep her upright, the support of Zach's heated body completely gone.

Kat recognized the two men holding Zach away from her, one on each side of him. Drew Winston looked immaculate in an expensive suit and tie, but Hunter was dressed casually in a black t-shirt and jeans, his face covered in cuts and bruises, looking like he'd just been through a war zone.

"He wasn't hurting me," Kat protested breathlessly, her gaze focused on Zach, his glowing eyes making his expression feral as he jerked at his arms to get out of his brothers' hold.

The two men yanked Zach backward, shoving him none too gently into one of the chairs at the kitchen table.

"Rein it in, Zach. You can't do this with a rescue," Hunter growled as he kept a forceful hand on Zach's shoulder as Drew did the same on the other side. "You'll hate yourself for it later."

Drew's gaze trailed over Kat, finally meeting her eyes. "You okay?" he questioned kindly.

"Yes. Of course," she assured him, wishing they'd let go of Zach. For some reason, she hated to see him restrained. "Please let him go." She could feel Zach's desire to be free, and it clawed at her, made her want to try to fight the two men confining him.

*I'm okay, Kat. Don't worry. They're trying to help me. I lost control.* The comforting words flowed through her mind, calming her.

Her eyes were riveted on Zach as she watched his breathing return to normal and his eyes slowly change from amber to chocolate brown. At that moment, she knew how incredibly strong he was, his ability to fight off the pulverizing demon instincts that were inherent in him, speaking volumes about his strength of character, his humanity. She'd felt the full force of his raw instinct to get free, violently if needed, but he'd forced it back down, unwilling to hurt his own brothers.

His eyes met hers as he picked up her thoughts and said aloud, "Yeah, but I didn't do so well a few minutes ago. I'm sorry," he said with remorse, his fierce eyes meeting hers. Shrugging off his brothers' hold, he stood. "I'm good. Let go."

Drew and Hunter both stared at Zach skeptically, but they released him.

"What the hell were you doing? And what the hell was Kristoff thinking to send you on a rescue?" Drew demanded, his voice both angry and concerned. "I thought he was yanking our chain when he told us he sent you out on a rescue. Obviously he wasn't."

"You were both occupied. There wasn't anyone else," Zach answered, shooting Drew an annoyed look. "They would have taken Kat. There was no time."

"It's not like we're the only two rescuing Sentinels. There are others," Hunter scoffed. "What was your bargain for the rescue? And why in the hell is she here?"

Zach's brows drew together, his expression fierce. "It's…complicated."

Kat looked from Zach to his two brothers and back again. Zach was blocking his thoughts from her now, but it was pretty evident that he was basically telling them to shut the hell up. And honestly, she wanted to tell them the same thing. How dare they come here and belittle what Zach had done for her?

She stalked up to Drew and jabbed a finger into his chest. "He rescued me, saved my life. Don't you dare criticize him. I agreed to the same thing that the evil demons wanted."

Drew stared down at her, his brow raising and his lips twitching slightly, as though he were amused. "And what was that?" Kat noticed vaguely that Drew had a rather attractive lilt to his voice, a bit of a Scottish or Irish accent, but she was too irritated to dwell on it.

"One week of my time doing anything Zach wants. Not a bad bargain since he smells better than they do and he doesn't want to torture and kill me," she told him sarcastically, not sure she liked either of Zach's brothers. She owed Zach her life, and they were chastising him?

Hunter exploded. "What the fuck, man?" He ran a frustrated hand through his hair. Pacing the kitchen, he said irritably, "You don't need that for a Sentinel bargain. Shit, you could have taken a penny, a lock of her hair…or any damn thing you wanted. Why a week of servitude? That's just crazy." He stopped pacing and stopped next to Zach, drilling him with an intense stare. "Why?"

"I asked for it, okay? I screwed up," Zach growled back at Hunter. "I'm a damn recruiter, not a rescuer."

"But it's not like you didn't know that you can take anything. You might not be trained in rescues, but you know the damn basics. What the hell?"

Drew coughed loudly and folded his arms in front of him, his gaze moving from Zach to Kat before speaking. "Uh…Hunter…I think you're missing something significant here."

"What?" Hunter's eyes flew to Drew, his voice impatient.

Drew smirked as he said casually, "What would compel Zach to ask for *that*? Think about it." He lifted his hand and placed it lightly on Kat's shoulder, looking deliberately at Zach as he did it.

"Don't. Touch. Her." Zach's guttural voice vibrated through the kitchen.

Kat's eyes flew to his face, stunned by his tone that was…well…demonic.

Drew removed his hand immediately, a satisfied look on his face.

"Fuck!" Hunter exclaimed loudly, flinching as he ran his hand across his face, obviously irritating the cuts and bruises on his skin. "She's his damn *radiant*." He sank into the chair closest to him, gaping at Kat and Zach, his expression stunned.

"You're right, Zach." Drew sat as he spoke, crossing his arms in front of him and arching a dark brow as he looked at Zach. "That's complicated."

*What in the hell is a radiant...and why is it complicated?*

Kat frowned, watching the three brothers as she tried to figure out what was happening.

"Can someone please explain this to me?" Kat asked, exasperated. She was tired and emotionally overwhelmed, and it had been a long and terrifying day. Really, all she wanted to do was crawl into bed, pull the covers over her head, and sleep for a week. "I was going to make a deal with evil demons. Zach saved me. Why is that such a terrible thing? And what exactly is a *radiant*?"

"What? You haven't told her?" Drew asked Zach with a frown.

"Not yet. I haven't had a chance," Zach answered, shooting a warning look at his brother.

"Maybe you should have mentioned it before you stuck your tongue down her throat," Hunter mumbled, disgruntled.

Kat's face flushed, remembering the heated embrace that had been abruptly interrupted by Zach's brothers. "Mentioned what exactly?" she mumbled, embarrassed.

"Leave. Now. I want to talk to Kat alone," Zach grunted to his brothers.

Hunter and Drew exchanged a knowing look and nodded.

"Before we leave, you need to know that something's up. We've lost a few who were under our protection," Drew said gravely, his whole demeanor changing to one of remorse.

"Lost them how?" Zach rumbled.

"We don't know." Drew shook his head as he added, "Somehow the Evils are breaking our protection, getting our previous rescues to agree to go with them to their own doom. It doesn't make sense. These are people who know the truth. Only one incident was actually seen by one of our guardians. From his description, it sounds like Goran and some of the ancients."

"It's a power play. I'll kill every one of the ugly bastards. They want to prove they can outmaneuver us," Hunter snarled, his eyes glowing with hatred.

"You aren't doing any of us any good when you keep ending up like you are now," Drew answered dryly. "Try playing by the rules for a change."

"I do. My rules," Hunter answered belligerently, disappearing as the words left his mouth.

Drew shook his head slowly at Hunter's disappearing form before turning his attention back to Zach. "Be careful. We aren't sure what's up but I'll keep you informed," Drew told Zach as his eyes drifted to Kat and pinned her with an intense look. "Be good to him. He needs you."

Kat took a deep breath as Drew's form faded, leaving her staring at the kitchen wall. Three Sentinels in one room had been intense, even if they were sort of the good guys. Strangely, the volatile atmosphere in the room was no less acute, power vibrating from Zach as he clamped his hands on her shoulders and turned her toward him.

His expression fierce, his eyes piercing her with raw emotion, he told her in a husky voice, "A *radiant* is the demon equivalent of a chosen mate. When the gods created the Sentinels, they gave us one opportunity to lighten the darkness of our souls. Our *radiant* is our only chance."

*I'm his mate. I'm Zach's mate?*

Kat should have been astounded, or at least extremely surprised. But…she wasn't. Somewhere deep inside herself…she recognized the truth. She could feel it, had felt the pull of her soul to his almost from the moment she saw him. Maybe, even before that, when her eyes had kept drifting back to his picture in the Winston building, her reaction to the sorrow in his eyes slamming her in the gut every time she looked at his image. "What happens now?" she asked him curiously.

Every muscle in his face tensed and his expression turned tormented. Kat wanted to soothe him, hold him until his pain went away. Yes,

Zach's soul was dark, but it wasn't all caused by his demon heritage. Kat knew he was hanging on to some sort of remorse, something festering inside him that needed to be healed.

"Nothing." Zach dropped his hands from her shoulders and shook his head. "Nothing can happen. You're under a demon bargain, compulsions that you can't deny. You don't want me, Kat. You don't want to be the *radiant* to a demon. I lost control earlier. I'm sorry," he told her softly, his voice resigned. "You look exhausted. Let's get some sleep."

As he turned to walk away, Kat's entire being rebelled, clamoring for her to comfort him, to take away the emptiness inside him that gnawed at her until she almost couldn't bear it. Following behind him, she acknowledged that her need had nothing to do with his wants or his compulsions. They were completely and utterly her own.

# Chapter Five

K at stood between the two demons, her whole body trembling with confusion. Neither demon was touching her, leaving a few feet of space on each side, but both were trying to gain control of her. Her decision should have been easy. Zach was on her right, and a large evil demon, bigger than Dwarf or Goblin but just as hideous, was on her left.

She stepped toward Zach, but every emotion inside her rebelled, telling her not to let him take her. Why? She trusted Zach completely. He'd saved her life. She had no reason to fear him. But as she tried to move again, she was bombarded by the same internal alarms, her body stopping after a slight step in his direction.

Something was wrong. Terribly wrong.

Kat's eyes flew to Zach's face, and then she knew. It was Zach…yet not. His eyes were bloodshot and glowing a dull red. The difference was subtle, but it was there.

Tearing her eyes away from Zach's beckoning form, she looked at the Evil, his eyes glowing amber, drawing her to him for some unknown reason.

Panicked, she looked from one demon to the other; what she saw was completely different from what her gut was telling her. How was it that the Evil actually felt safe while Zach repulsed her?

*"Come with me. Offer your life and I'll make sure your nephew is safe. Agree now,"* Zach demanded, his voice grating and so unlike his usual smooth, husky baritone.

*Kat took a small step in the other direction, toward the Evil, but no alarm bells were going off in her head, no shiver traveling down her spine. The closer she moved toward the troll demon, the safer she felt.*

*It made no sense, and she shook her head, unable to decipher why she wasn't moving toward Zach, getting away from the Evil. She'd give her life for her nephew without regret, but she needed to be certain that it would keep him safe, and she wasn't so positive that giving her life for Stevie's was going to keep him alive. Hadn't Zach already told her that her nephew was safe? Why was he asking her for something more?*

*Knowing her gut feeling was correct, she said aloud, "No. You're not Zach. He'd never ask that of me. And I can sense you're not him."*

*"Stupid bitch," the pseudo-Zach snarled. He lunged toward her, arms reaching out to grab her. Scrambling to avoid his grasp, she tripped and fell on her ass right beside the Evil.*

*The Evil suddenly moved for the first time, vaulting into action by yanking her behind him, and springing toward the Zach look-alike, putting himself between her and the demon trying to attack her. It was as if the Evil were actually trying to protect her.*

*Disoriented, dazed and terrified, Kat let loose a bloodcurdling scream as the two demons collided, not even completely sure which one she wanted to win the battle.*

Zach woke from his nightmare to the sound of Kat's scream. His heart was pumping as he tried to shake off the bad dream he'd been having, a common occurrence that plagued Sentinels, his main concern being what was happening to Kat.

Transporting himself to the guest room, his chest heaving with fear and from the residual adrenaline from his nightmare, he arrived at Kat's bedside scared shitless. Her body was thrashing violently on the bed as she whimpered, her eyes still closed.

*Fuck.*

"Kat." Sitting down on the bed, he grasped her arms and sat her up, shaking her gently. She remained asleep, her head tilting sideways, and Zach got more desperate. "Kat. Open your eyes," he repeated sternly, bellowing the command.

Her eyes popped open suddenly, as she gave an audible gasp, and Zach frowned as she looked at him with obvious terror and started struggling to break his hold.

"Stop. Kat. You were dreaming," he told her in a soothing voice, not at all liking her beautiful green eyes filled with trepidation as she looked at him.

"Zach? Is it really you?" she asked, her voice soft and hesitant.

"Yeah." *Who in the hell did she think he was?*

"Can you turn on the light?" she requested quietly. She had stopped struggling, but she was tense, her body stiff.

Zach activated the light by the bedside with his magic, momentarily forgetting that Kat didn't have perfect sight in the dark. Still, he would have thought she would recognize his voice.

*And my touch.*

He could understand her waking up confused and scared from a bad dream, but she seemed terrified *of him.* "Kat, I would never hurt you," he told her gravely, disappointed that she would have any doubts about him, but he supposed she had good reason after the scene in the kitchen.

She blinked as her eyes adjusted to the light, her gaze flying up to meet his, searching for…something. "Oh, thank God. It's you," she said, throwing her arms around his neck with a sigh of relief.

His arms tightened around her reflexively, his protective, possessive instincts barely held in check as he cradled her soft, feminine body against him. "Who the hell else would I be?" he asked her in a disgruntled voice. Granted, they had only known each other for less than a day, but it still bugged him that she wasn't as hyper-aware of him as he was of her. "What were you dreaming about?" he asked her in a gentler voice as he felt her trembling in his arms. *Jesus, it must have been some fucking nightmare.*

"I was dreaming about you, except it wasn't you. You were an Evil and the Evil was you," she answered in a muffled voice against his shoulder. "You asked me to give my life for my nephew. But it wasn't you. And it didn't make any sense. You said Stevie was safe." She was babbling, her explanation confusing, but it was obvious that she meant every word she uttered.

"He is safe." Zach should have discounted what she was saying as complete nonsense, but his body tensed as he realized that she had been having much the same dream as he. Except the Evil had been an ancient, the gray tufts of hair and larger size identifying his age. The ugly bastard had looked exactly like what it was…a very old Evil. Still, it was strange that Kat had been experiencing a similar dream, one where an Evil had been trying to get her to agree to a life bargain. In his dream, Kat had been hesitant, not immediately choosing to come to him. He had been mute, unable to speak, the helplessness nearly driving him insane. He had also been paralyzed, unable to move until Kat had chosen not to accept the bargain. All he had been able to do was observe until she had rejected the Evil. "You refused the Evil. You chose me. Even though I looked like an Evil?"

"I didn't choose you. I moved toward the Evil and fell," she said, her voice confused. "Were you there?"

*Drew said that the Evils were somehow taking humans under Sentinel protection. Was it possible that they were doing it through the dream realm? Could I have been pulled into the dream as a Sentinel witness?*

It sounded implausible, but how could he and Kat be having such a similar dream without it being more than coincidence?

Zach's arms tightened around Kat. The possibility that what they had both experienced being more than just a bad dream was scaring the shit out of him. What if it had been more? What would have happened had Kat not refused? "Are you saying that the demon offering to take your life for your nephew's looked like me?"

She pulled back and looked at him. "Yes. He looked exactly like you, except his eyes were glowing red and I sensed it wasn't you. The Evils have come to me through dreams before, but not quite like this. They were showing me scenarios of what could happen to Stevie, breaking me down through my nightmares."

"Fuck." *The bastards.* Somehow they *were* manipulating dreams.

He manifested his cell phone and drew one hand away from Kat to punch in Kristoff's number, keeping his other arm tightly around her.

When Kristoff answered in an irritated voice, the call clearly having woken him, Zach simply grumbled, "I need all of you. Now." Punching the Off button, he got rid of the phone, and waited, his body tense.

"Zach, what's happening?" Kat questioned, her voice frightened.

He ran a hand down his face in frustration, hoping his suspicions were wrong. "I'm not sure. I need to talk to Kristoff, Drew, and Hunter."

"Zach?" she murmured.

"Yeah?" He tightened his arms around her, needing to reassure himself that Kat was okay and comfort her fears, even though they may very well be justified.

"Do you realize you're…um…naked?" She drew her hand down his bare back slowly and to his hip, caressing his naked flesh.

"Am I now?" he answered hoarsely, his eyes closing for a brief moment while he savored the feel of her soft hand drifting over his bare skin, the sensation having nothing to do with her being his *radiant* and everything to do with the fact that Kat lightened his heart as well as his soul. Years of loneliness and regret faded in her presence and the feel of her hands on his body was pure bliss.

He could feel her warm breath against his ear as she whispered, "Feels like it to me." She stroked again, moving slower this time, her touch soft and light.

Zach slammed his mind closed, unwilling to let Kat sense that her touch was making him want…and…want…and…want.

Clothing himself instantly, he mourned the feel of her softness against his naked flesh and sighed before answering, "Don't want the guys to get jealous of my superior man parts."

Kat laughed softly, the light feminine sound vibrating against his ear. *Mine. My radiant. My mate.*

Zach tried to shove down his demon instincts that were clawing to the surface. He wanted Kat more than he had ever wanted anything, but it was a selfish need, and he knew it.

*I'm not bonding her to me. I'm not making her my radiant. She's had enough darkness in her life. She doesn't need any of mine.*

"I thought you said you needed us." His king's voice was displeased, but as Zach pulled away from Kat to look at Kristoff and his two brothers flanking their ruler, all of them had concerned looks on their faces.

Zach turned toward the arrivals, but he wrapped an arm around Kat, keeping her cradled protectively at his side. "I think the Evils are making life bargains in the dream realm with people under our protection, nullifying our bargains and stealing them away," he told them, watching as his two brothers looked at him in disbelief. Hell, he couldn't blame them. It sounded crazy to him too, but he had experienced it. They hadn't.

"Not possible. Nothing nullifies a Sentinel bargain," Hunter grumbled.

"Are you sure you're okay, Zach?" Drew mumbled, his brows drawing together, examining Zach as though trying to assess his mental state. "You know that's not possible."

"Actually…it is possible," Kristoff muttered, stepping forward and crossing his arms in front of him. "Highly unlikely, but not exactly impossible." He moved then, crouching down next to Kat and bringing her eyes level with his. "I'd like to look at your dreams, Kat. I'm Kristoff, king of the Sentinels. I want to see if this was just a dream or if it could be an Evil dream invasion. Will you let me?"

"It's not the first time the Evils have invaded her dreams. Her visions of what could happen to her nephew were actually nightmares manifested in the dream realm," Zach informed Kristoff, his fury at the fact that the Evils had invaded her sleep, a time when she was so incredibly vulnerable, making him nearly insane.

"I'd like to look, Kat. See the dreams from your perspective. May I?" Kristoff queried gently.

Zach knew his king could simply take the memories, invade Kat's mind without asking permission, but as much as Kristoff might annoy him at times, Zach admired the Sentinel demon king's inherent kindness with innocent humans.

"I didn't know you had to ask. Zach doesn't. But if it will help you, be my guest," Kat replied, staring at Kristoff with a little more admiration than Zach liked.

"You're Zach's *radiant* and your thoughts flow to him automatically. It's natural," Kristoff replied. "But I'll have to probe and look in your mind, and it might be a little uncomfortable, but it won't be painful. I promise."

Zach's chest ached as Kat looked up at him for reassurance, her trust in him nearly taking his breath away. He nodded and took her fragile hand in his, twining their fingers together, wishing that Kristoff could just take the information from him. Unfortunately, his king wouldn't see the dream the way Kat had experienced it. "He can't get the information from me," he told her flatly. "I'm sorry." He could read her memories easily because she was his *radiant*, but Kristoff needed to see the information firsthand.

Kat turned her eyes back to Kristoff. "Then do it. If it helps other people from suffering a terrible fate, a little discomfort is nothing."

The demon king nodded once, giving Kat a reassuring smile, and his eyes immediately began to glow. Unlike other Sentinels, Kristoff's eyes were a deep sapphire blue, lightening to the color of a clear sky and emitting a hazy, pale light as he shuffled through Kat's memories, frowning as he pulled the information he needed from her, taking the time he needed to avoid disorienting Kat.

Zach felt Kat shiver, knowing she wasn't in pain, but could definitely feel the sensation of Kristoff searching, moving in her brain. Searching for memories was different from reading a human's thoughts. It took longer, more exploration, and while it wasn't painful, he hated the fact that Kristoff was in Kat's head. Since she was his *radiant*, he could search her mind effortlessly, but any other person rifling through her memories would cause her discomfort.

*Mine.*

Clenching his hand on his thigh, he tried to relinquish the possessiveness he felt toward her, but it wasn't possible. Every minute it grew more difficult, more suffocating, his demon instincts insisting that he claim his *radiant* and protect her from anyone who threatened her in any way.

Kristoff broke contact with Kat and stood, his face stoic as his eyes returned to their normal dark blue. Zach hated himself when he had to swallow a growl as Kristoff caught Kat's hand and squeezed it briefly before he stood, a gesture of gratitude and thanks. A Sentinel couldn't stand anyone of the opposite sex touching their radiant until after they had bonded, and even then, it was barely tolerable.

"She saw the Evil as Zach," Kristoff said thoughtfully before continuing, "But because she's Zach's *radiant*, she could sense the difference. It was more than just a nightmare. The Evils were present."

"But how can a dream bargain nullify a Sentinel agreement?" Hunter asked with his usual surliness.

Kristoff sighed heavily as he scowled at Hunter. "He wanted a life bargain. The only thing that can nullify a Sentinel bargain is to make a life bargain with an Evil, something that is never ordinarily done because anyone under our protection knows the Evil won't honor it. Life bargains have never been an issue before. Evils invading dreams haven't been an issue either, but obviously they've discovered a way to do it."

"But bargains in the dream realm aren't valid," Drew argued, folding his arms in front of him, shifting irritably. "And a Sentinel has to be witness to a life bargain with an Evil to nullify Sentinel protection. It's never happened. It doesn't happen."

Kristoff shrugged, but he looked far from nonchalant. "It's a gray area. The bargain could be obtained in the dream realm with a Sentinel witness who thinks he's simply having one of our frequent nightmares. Somehow they are able to lull a sleeping Sentinel into the dream as an observer. An Evil could snatch the human, wake him or her, and verify consent on the human plane of existence while that person is still muddled. The bargain would hold if it's verified immediately while the person is awake."

Drew cursed under his breath before commenting, "But the Evils wouldn't be able to hold their illusion-"

"After the victim was awake?" Kristoff raised a brow. "Under the cover of darkness, how are they to know? We know only a life bargain can get around our protection. Do you have a better theory as to how we're losing humans under our protection?"

"Shit! No, I don't. I sure as hell wish I did. How do we combat this? The ugly little bastards are trying to prove their strength by taking our rescues. They're even able to draw one of us in to witness so it's valid," Drew replied, his jaw clenched, his eyes beginning to take on an amber glow.

"I'll get a message to all Sentinel regional leaders and let them know what's happening, emphasize that they need to pay attention to any nightmares that are similar to what Zach and Kat experienced. The guardians need to be on high alert and aware that the Evils are able to enter the dreams of victims."

"We don't have enough guardians to watch every rescue," Hunter snarled as he pounded a fist into his palm, his agitation pulsating through the room, his eyes gleaming golden light.

"No, we don't. And we haven't figured out completely how this is happening. Every Sentinel is going to have to be vigilant," Kristoff asserted, his expression implacable, his innate instinct to protect humans clear from the fierce expression on his face. Turning to Zach, he pinned him with a commanding look. "You need to make a life bargain with Kat or bind her to you for her protection. It's the only way to keep her safe right now. It's highly possible the Evils will try again and there's no guarantee that you will be the witnessing Sentinel next time, although I suspect that the Evils need a sleeping, vulnerable Sentinel nearby to pull off this crap. They've obviously figured out how to bring a Sentinel into the dream realm as just a witness and keep them subdued unless they're denied. I noticed in Kat's dream that you weren't able to make a move until she refused the Evil."

All the breath whooshed out of Zach's lungs at Kristoff's statement. "I can't make her my *radiant*. She doesn't deserve that. You know what has to happen and what she's already been through," Zach growled back at Kristoff. No matter how much his demon nature clamored for her to belong to him, he wasn't taking her. His darkness was too black, too suffocating.

"She wouldn't be your *radiant* if she couldn't handle it. Goddammit, Zach, this is no time for you to have your head up your ass by lamenting over what you think are mistakes in your past. You need to look to Kat's safety. Make a life bargain with her…or I will. She can still be set free after the bargain and retain our protection."

Zach looked up at Kristoff, wanting to go for his throat. This wasn't about past mistakes or insecurities. This was about Kat, a woman he could see from the inside out, a woman who had spent her whole adult life caring for others and asking for nothing for herself. She gave… and… gave…and gave, until Zach wasn't sure how she had anything left to give. How could he take the rest of her life from her?

*I could set her free if I made a life bargain, give her everything she needs to live her life the way she deserves.*

There was no fucking way he was letting Kristoff make the bargain with her. Just the thought of another man being able to control how Kat lived her life sickened him, demon king or not. It had nothing to do with trust. He'd put *his* life in Kristoff's hands. But not Kat's.

*Mine.*

"I'll do it," he replied adamantly, knowing Kat needed protection, unable to let anyone else but him provide it. He didn't trust anyone else to look out for her the way he would. She needed a life bargain to protect her, and he didn't want her bound in any way to another male.

Problem was, he wasn't sure he trusted himself either. Once Kat had bargained her entire life to him, how in the hell would he ever let her go?

# Chapter Six

The next day, Zach wondered absently if a demon could do himself harm from whacking off so many times in such a short period of time. He had lost track of how many times he had taken himself in hand during the short duration that he'd known Kat, to take himself out of a state of arousal in order to keep Kat from feeling his compulsions. She was rapidly driving him completely insane.

She'd made a life bargain with him without hesitation after Kristoff, Drew, and Hunter had left during the night. The swiftness with which she'd agreed had humbled him, her trust in him so damn undeserved. The life bargain would protect her from all Evils unless something happened to him, but the terms of the initial bargain still had to be fulfilled.

*Six more days of this fucking torture. Six more days of trying to block my wants.*

Unfortunately, he was utterly and completely fixated on Kat, his wants all revolving around her. Anything else he wanted could easily be hidden from her, but his need for her was nearly impossible to control.

With her being under the control of the bargain she'd made…he could have taken her any way he wanted to. Unfortunately, the man in him wouldn't allow himself to do it. Taking his woman under compulsion wouldn't give him satisfaction. It might appease his demon nature, but he would be disgusted with himself.

He twirled his glass of whiskey, watching the ice circle in the glass. Could he handle six more days of this constant wanting? He shifted positions on the couch in his spacious den, trying to get comfortable, which was damn difficult when his cock was nearly always standing at attention.

Six more days of the initial demon bargain, but she wouldn't have to be with him for the life bargain…if he set her free to live her own life. The life agreement would last the duration of her human years, would protect her even though she wasn't near him physically…though he would never be free of Kat, of wanting her, needing her. That thought nearly rubbed his emotions raw. He was getting addicted to her company, and his sexual urges were driving him mad.

Afraid to let her out of his sight after their shared nightmare, Zach had taken her to his bed and held her, both of them talking about anything and everything as he held her close to reassure himself that she was safe. Kat loved history, and when she found out how old he was, she had begged for every story he could tell her about significant events in the last two hundred years. She never seemed to run out of questions and he never tired of hearing her voice.

*She's a balm for my loneliness, a light to my darkness. Mine. My radiant.*

Zach tossed back a swallow of whiskey, feeling the burn of the liquid as it flowed slowly down his throat. Demons couldn't get drunk…but they could appreciate the taste of a great Scotch.

He smiled as he thought about how Kat had shooed him out of his own home office a few minutes ago, claiming that he was distracting her while she worked on the computer to do some of her business paperwork. Her sister Nora was covering her jobs this week, Kat having told her sibling that she was taking a vacation. *Oh yeah, fun in the dark demon realm with soul sucking Evils. That would have been relaxing.* Zach shook his head and took another sip of alcohol, trying to let the burn make him forget what Kat would be suffering right now had he not rescued her. Did the woman not have any sense of self-preservation?

She beguiled and fascinated him…and not just because she was his *radiant.* Any woman who gave up her entire life for two of her relatives was nearly a saint in his eyes. The human women he knew-mostly the women he had fucked-wouldn't give five minutes for any problem but their own, and their idea of a tragedy was generally a broken nail right after a manicure. Kat had been a history major in college and had dropped everything to help her twin and her nephew. What kind of woman did something like that?

*Only Kat.*

On the flip side…the woman did have a temper and he had to admit that he liked to get her riled up just to see her green eyes flashing fire. She had an untapped passion that he was dying to wallow in. Everything about her delighted him, and that was an emotion that was completely new and intoxicating.

Kat attracted him like a moth to the light, making him constantly seek her out, eager for her warmth and illumination. His soul grew lighter every moment he spent in her presence and he was starting to get concerned that he wasn't going to be able to survive without her. Damn it…he already didn't want to be without her. The woman made him experience feelings that he hadn't experienced since becoming a demon. Actually, to be honest, he had never felt this way about a woman. Ever.

The fact that she actually didn't think she was attractive was almost unbelievable to Zach, because every single thing about her captivated him. He knew she was under that impression because he still read her thoughts. She was his *radiant* and her feelings and thoughts drifted into his mind as naturally as his own. Truthfully, he didn't want to block them. He allowed himself that one indulgence, aware that it annoyed Kat, but it took the edge off his demon side. If he couldn't bury himself in her body, at least he could hear her thoughts, and the intimacy soothed him.

Visions of Kat's face, her sharp green eyes and sensuous lips, formed in his mind. He wanted to have her in every possible way. The image shifted itself to Kat, on her knees, taking his cock into her mouth, stroking it with her tongue.

He lay back on the couch, his hand reaching automatically to free himself from his jeans. *Oh, Christ. Not again.* He was going to go blind.

He palmed himself as his eyes closed and he stopped fighting the onset of the fantasy…only one of many that he'd had during the day.

He never heard her enter the room. Abandoned to his fantasy, he wasn't aware of her presence until he felt her hand over his, tugging to take it away from his cock.

He opened his eyes…and there was his gorgeous Kat, her face strained and her gaze full of desire. She was pale and he wanted to curse himself for not knowing she was near.

*The bargain.*

*The compulsion.*

*She feels my desires and it's hurting her.*

He started to get up but she pushed him back down. "Please, Zach. Let me."

The will to resist left him as his demon demands took control. There was no way he could resist the pleading look in her beautiful green eyes. His hands fell to his sides as he felt the first incredible touch of her soft fingers.

"You're so big." Her voice was breathy and sultry. Zach trembled as Kat slid her palm up and down the shaft like she was learning the feel and texture of him.

He propped his head up on a pillow to watch her face. When she tilted her head down and slowly undulated her tongue over his begging tip, he nearly exploded like an untried schoolboy. The feel of her tongue on his cock was exquisite. He groaned as it twitched, pleading for her hot mouth. She was killing him, but he'd gladly expire if *this* was the way he was going to leave the Earth realm.

Zach wanted to grasp Kat's hair and thrust himself into her mouth, but he willed himself to stay patient as he watched her tongue glide sensuously along his swollen tip, causing his balls to tighten and his hips to pump.

He groaned as he felt her lips slide over the head and take as much of his shaft as she could handle. He could feel the friction against her tongue and the roof of her mouth. After so many fantasies, the reality and erotic feel of her were almost surreal.

"I won't last long, Kat," he panted as she started a suction that nearly made him explode, the pleasure of her movements so intense that he could already feel his building orgasm.

Out of his mind with lust, Zach thrust his hand into that long, silky hair and guided her to a faster rhythm, needing the intense pace. Desire surged with a speed that was almost brutal, and he needed the ruthless strokes more than he needed the next beat of his heart. The visual of her lips sucking and her head bobbing up and down on his cock was as heady as the feel of her mouth and tongue against his member. She was taking what belonged to her, and Zach reveled in it.

"Mmmmm…." Her lips vibrated against him, adding more stimulation to the already mind-blowing pleasure.

Had anything in his entire existence ever felt this good? He wanted to make it last, savor the pleasure, but it was just too intense.

"Kat. Fuck. I'm ready to explode." Zach couldn't hold back. She needed to take those lips from him before he choked her with his violent release.

Kat didn't move her mouth. She nearly swallowed him. As he felt his cock hit the back of her throat, encompassed in the hot, wet suction… he detonated.

Zach cursed as his orgasm took control. His back arched at the ecstasy of releasing himself into the warm, tight cavern as she swallowed his seed like it was ambrosia.

*Holy shit!* His legs were still trembling as her tongue stroked over his cock, licking every drop of his release, and it was the most erotic thing he'd ever seen.

Zach reached down, picked Kat up and pulled her over him like a blanket. He wrapped his arms around her and held her soft body against his. He wished they were naked, wanting to feel her soft skin against him without any barriers. His arms held her tightly, her head resting on his shoulder.

"Zach, I'm too heavy to lie on top of you." Kat squirmed to get away, but she didn't stand a chance against his demon hold.

*Seriously? I'm a damn demon, and she's not heavy anyway.* He gave her a playful slap on the ass and she stopped. "You feel like perfection." A thought danced through his mind of her on top of him, riding them both into oblivion. She'd look beautiful, wild and moaning his name as she climaxed.

*Awww…hell.* He slammed the fantasy thought closed as a twinge of guilt hit him in the gut.

As though she could read his thoughts, Kat answered, "I did that because I wanted to, not because I had to." Her voice was muffled against his shoulder.

Zach stroked her hair as he replied, "You needed to. It's the damn bargain." It pissed him off. He had just had the most incredible orgasm of his life…and his woman had done it because of demon compulsion.

She pulled back and met his eyes. "I wanted to. Yes, I felt compelled, but I also want you. I wasn't forced."

He didn't believe her. Demon compulsions were strong. She didn't know the difference between being compelled and wanting it herself.

He tried to explain to her, but she insisted, "Zach…you already got off. My panties are soaked and I want you so badly that my whole body aches. The urges to satisfy you are nothing compared to my own desires. Does the bargain include me burning with need even after you just came?"

*Hell no, it didn't.* The bargain only compelled *her* to satisfy *him.* "You want me?"

"Demon…I want you so badly right now I want to rip your clothes off and satisfy myself a hundred different ways." Kat sighed. "I think I'll go take a shower." She sounded flustered and embarrassed by her confession.

She started to move off him, but Zach clamped his arms around her waist, keeping her tightly against him, his heart hammering with hope.

He delved into her mind, reading every emotion. Strange, he had always figured those thoughts were his alone, compulsions or part of the demon bargain.

They weren't.

Kat should be feeling satisfied that she had temporarily sated him. But he could feel nothing but yearning, her need for him, her own fantasies.

Zach grinned at her as he took in the fact that this hadn't all been coerced on her part. "You have some very naughty fantasies, Kitten." And damned if he didn't want to act out every one of them, satisfy her until she begged for mercy. She was the one wanting now, and he was going to be the man to take care of every one of her needs.

She gave him an exasperated expression. "Zach, I just wanted you to know that it wasn't forced. I wanted you to understand."

He ran his hand over her ass, squeezing each cheek as he pulled her hips to his. "Oh, I understand perfectly now. I'm glad you explained it."

Kat actually wanted him. Not because she was under a bargain or because she was compelled. She really wanted *him*.

Zach laughed as he sat up, scooping her up with him.

"Zach...what are you doing?" Her voice sounded panicked.

Now that he knew that she needed him, there was nothing that could stop him. And it was way past time for her to realize how beautiful she was, how completely irresistible.

Zach laughed as Kat kicked her feet, trying to get him to put her down. He just held her tighter and sprinted up the stairs, his only want-his greatest need-to satisfy his mate.

# Chapter Seven

Kat stopped worrying about Zach carrying her generously curved body when he reached the top of the stairs. He wasn't even out of breath. *Holy crap...this demon was strong.*

What in the hell was he up to? She shouldn't have confessed her desire for him, but she didn't want him feeling guilty. She had started to care for him and she didn't want him beating himself up for something that she had enjoyed. She knew he already flogged himself enough over past mistakes. In the darkness of the night, he had told her about his sister, his mother-his regrets. They had shared a lot during those intimate hours together, and Zack had kept her safe in his warm embrace.

As he slowly lowered her to her feet in the master bedroom, she eyed him nervously. "What are you doing?"

Kat backed up, but her ass hit the oak bedpost. She wasn't sure she liked his slightly evil grin. It made her heart flip and her mouth go dry. Surely he wasn't considering...

"Kitten, there's no way I'm letting you go into the shower by yourself." His voice was graveled as his arm snaked around her waist. "I plan on joining you. I'm sure you can feel what I want right now."

She did...and it sent tingles down her spine, in addition to other places on her body. "Why?" Okay...she didn't understand this, and she wanted to. Zach's desire was real, and it was a rampant, uncontrolled, desire that she just couldn't comprehend. "I'm not attractive, Zach. I'm not saying that because my self-esteem is low or because I'm insecure. It's just a fact. My face is plain and if you look close enough, you can see freckles. I'm plump by today's standards for how a woman should look, and I'm nothing any man desires this much. I'm intelligent, I'm a hard worker, and I'm a survivor…but I am not physically attractive to most men. Especially not to a man like you." Kat sucked in a deep breath as she finished, feeling strangely comfortable revealing how she felt to Zach.

He crowded her, pushing her back and ass against the sturdy bedpost and trapping both her arms over her head, gripping them both snugly with one strong hand. His eyes were fierce and beginning to glow amber as he captured her gaze. "I'm not looking at you as just a man; I see you as a Sentinel demon views his *radiant*. I don't see insignificant flaws, things you view as unattractive…I see your fucking soul, and its lightness enthralls my darkness. I don't know how human men see you, and I don't give a damn as long as they don't touch you. My vision goes deeper, seeing you from the inside out, and what's inside you warms me, makes me want to find every freckle on your body so I can worship it. Your softness makes me want to bury myself inside you so deeply that neither one of us can do anything except get lost in the other, joined so tightly that we don't know where one stops and the other begins. I want that with a need so profound that it's nearly killing me. There's not one thing about you that isn't absolute perfection." He lowered his head, his mouth so close to her ear that she could feel his hot breath against the sensitive flesh as he rumbled in a low voice, "So don't tell me that you aren't beautiful. To me, you're the most exquisite female on the planet, and there'll never be another. Understand?"

Kat was mesmerized by his hypnotic voice and heartfelt declaration. Hard as it might be to believe…he meant every word. She could sense it, feel the truth of his words in her gut. It was hard to wrap her mind around the fact that someone who looked like Zach wanted her so desperately, but it was a heady feeling, one she had never experienced before. "I'm not used to it," she admitted in a breathy voice.

"Get used to it," he warned in a husky voice. "I'll never see you any other way."

Kat gulped as Zach released her and whipped his t-shirt over his head, baring his upper body. She quivered as his sexual needs consumed her. "You're doing that on purpose. Letting me feel your wants."

"Damn right, I am. I'm not even trying to hold back on thinking about what I want right now. I want you to feel it. I want you to own it. Because you're the only woman who's ever made me this insane. And I think it's time for you to understand just how much I want you and just how much I want to satisfy *your* needs." His jeans and briefs were gone seconds later and he was gloriously nude, looking better than in her wildest fantasies.

His body was perfect, every muscle sculpted and defined, his enormous cock nestled against his rock hard abs. He could have been carved from marble, but she knew he wasn't. Zach's body was hot and alive, and so incredibly responsive to her touch. She'd just experienced the truth of that on the couch downstairs.

Kat's brain was bombarded with scenes of them wet and naked, which she struggled and failed to contain. Protesting as he pulled her lightweight shirt over her head was out of the question. His greatest need right now was to have her naked and wet...and she couldn't fight against his desire. It was her desire, too, and her inexperience warred with overwhelming passion, but desire squelched the negative voices. Raw need was stronger, more powerful, impossible to deny.

Kat had little time for internal struggle-Zach had her naked so fast that she didn't have time to think for long.

His eyes lit with unmasked desire as he slowly devoured her with his head-to-toe appraisal. No man had ever looked at her this way. She had never imagined a man surveying her in a completely carnal manner-like he was consumed by hunger and wanted to have *her* for dinner...and dessert.

He pulled her willing body toward the master bathroom, one that she hadn't used before. It was designed exactly the same as the one attached to the guest room she was using.

The Jacuzzi shower was running, obviously adjusted by Zach's demon magic. It was turned to her favorite rainfall ceiling setting, with circular lights that gave the shower a romantic, dreamy atmosphere.

Zach pulled her into the enclosure and closed the door as he murmured, "I don't think we need to turn on the steam. I have plans to produce enough of our own."

Kat's breath sawed in and out of her lungs as he pulled her against him, skin to skin, and kissed her with an intensity that sucked the air from her lungs. Arms around her waist, he conquered her mouth, weaving their tongues together in an intimate dance. He was all raw male dominance, and she gave in to her urge to let herself be conquered by him.

His hands glided along her wet skin, sending a shiver down her spine. As his mouth moved to her ear, she heard him rasp, "My greatest need right now is to hear you moaning my name as you come." His hand snaked between her legs, causing her to gasp as his fingers slid dominantly between her tights. "So hot, so wet. I can feel your need, read your desire, and it's driving me insane." Kat moaned as his fingers stroked effortlessly through her slick folds, seeking and finding her clit. His mouth moved to her ample breasts, nipping and tugging at her already hard, sensitive nipples. He bit gently and soothed with his tongue, the pleasure/pain sensation making her begin to unravel.

"Please." Kat wasn't sure what she was begging for, but she was getting the double whammy as his needs and hers combined, making her body ignite and her pussy quiver. Zach's driving need at the moment was to make her climax intensely, over and over.

His eyes were amber and bright as he pulled his head back to look at her. He turned her, angling her back against his chest as he lifted her leg to place it onto a large, built-in seat.

Zach fell to his knees, pulling Kat's other leg out so that she was spread wide and vulnerable.

Whimpering helplessly as his fingers again began their assault on her pussy from behind, Kat's hands slapped against the wall in front of her to keep from tumbling over.

His need to satisfy her.

Her need for release.

Both bombarded her as he slipped two fingers into her empty channel, stroking in and out in a deep, slow rhythm that only increased her frustration. "Please, Zach." She was nearly sobbing for release and she pounded the wall with her fists as he worked his fingers in and out of her channel, stroking deeply, caressing a g-spot she had never known she had.

It was too much. Too much. Too much sensation, too much pleasure. Zach's hand spread her folds, exposing her clit.

The shower changed from a light rainfall to a true Jacuzzi jet spray and her clit was right in the path of one of the powerful massage jets.

"Zach! Oh, God." Kat was screaming at the increased speed of his finger-fucking combined with the massaging warm water hitting her exposed nub. The pulsating water felt like a fast-moving tongue over her clit and Zach's penetrations were driving her mad.

Kat's climax hit like a tornado, ripping into her with a force that was out of control. Her body bucked and writhed as she whimpered and moaned. Her channel gripped Zach's fingers as he pumped hard and fast, his ministrations absolutely relentless. He had but one want at the moment, and that was to see her climax. Hard.

She came apart, not sure if she would ever be able to put the pieces back together. A flood of creamy release flowed over Zach's fingers and she heard a low growl as he caught her when her legs failed to keep her standing.

He swung her onto the seat that had previously been supporting her leg and spread her thighs apart. Resting against the back wall, she let her head fall back for support.

"I love feeling you come. You're so responsive to me. I have to taste your pleasure," he said harshly.

Dear God, her body had never responded this way, but then, she had also never been taken by a demon.

Zach was still kneeling, leaning over her spent body as he whispered roughly in her ear, "You haven't been taken, Kat. Not yet."

The shower returned to a rainfall as Zach lifted her legs up and buried his face between them with a snarl.

He lapped at her folds, tasting her climax, swallowing her essence. He took his time, laving her clit, exploring her tender flesh.

Kat's hips tried to lift to increase the erotic pressure. How was it possible to still need him so badly after what had just happened? Her body was again pleading for relief as she grasped his head and pulled his face closer, holding him tighter, plunging her fingers into his wet hair.

Zach's tongue meandered along her pulsating bud, lifting the protective hood, leaving her bare to him.

"I need to come, Zach. Please," Kat panted as she squirmed, her ass sliding on the slippery seat.

The moment his teeth nipped over her clit and his tongue vibrated over her naked bud, the spasms clenched her pussy, releasing another flood of release. "Ah, God...Zach. Yes." Her climax was violent, rolling over every inch of her body.

He sipped the juices that were a result of her ecstasy, groaning against her core.

Her head thrashed as she cried, "I didn't know. I didn't know."

Zach slid up her body and pulled her wet, trembling form against him. "Didn't know what, Kitten?"

She released a strangled sob. "That it could be so intense, that it could feel like that."

He held her tightly, and she knew he understood. He could catch her raging emotions and thoughts and figure it out. It was a relief not to try to explain it. She was too overwhelmed and she couldn't find the words.

Kat's body was completely limp, but her mind was reeling over the discovery that sexual acts could be that all-consuming, that mind-blowing.

She clenched Zach tightly against her body, mindless of the water flowing over them like a gentle rain. The only thing she felt was Zach.

Zach lifted her gently and stepped out of the shower. Sitting her in a chair, he toweled her dry and brushed her damp hair. After drying himself and shutting off the water, he scooped her up and deposited her in the bed. He spooned himself around her, pulling her body tightly against him.

She was just drifting off to sleep when she felt him bury his face in her damp hair, his breath warm against her neck as she thought she heard him murmur softly, "I didn't know either, Kat. It's never been like this for me. Not even close."

They were both asleep moments later.

# Chapter Eight

Kat fought against waking, happy in her warm cocoon of slumber, but the demands of her body wouldn't be ignored. It only took her a moment to realize why her body felt like it was being licked with flames of desire.

Feeling Zach's hard chest against her back, his hand caressing her nipples and his fingers teasing her damp folds, she knew exactly why she had to wake up. Her body was on fire...and so was Zach's.

She pushed back against his erect member, eliciting a low groan from him as he whispered in her ear, "Good morning."

The seductive tone only made her pussy spring forth more moisture as he rolled her onto her back. He dropped hot, open-mouthed kisses over her face and neck as he spread her legs wide and positioned himself between them. She could feel his enormous cock sliding up and down her slit, coating itself with her abundant fluid.

"I can't be patient, Kitten. I need this too much," he groaned, his face desperate.

Waiting was the last thing she wanted. No teasing, no tormenting. She just wanted him. She slid her arms around his neck, hungry to be filled. "Fuck me, Zach. Please."

He groaned as he slid the head inside her entrance and thrust. "Kat, you're so damn tight."

"I-I'm not very experienced." Would he be turned off by her lack of skill? Oh God…she hoped not. She wasn't used to someone of his size invading her channel, but it didn't hurt. It burned with an erotic sensation that incited her urgency to feel his cock inside her, deep and hard. Her primal need for him was raw and incredibly carnal.

"I don't want experience, but I don't want to hurt you. I just want to be inside you," Zach rasped as he stroked another inch and her pussy swallowed it.

"No control, demon. You don't need it. Just give it to me." Her hips rolled up and she planted her feet on the mattress. Her feet found purchase on the smooth, silk sheets and she met his next stroke with one of her own.

"Fuck!" Zach panted as he became buried inside her.

Kat moaned at the feel of his possession, her walls expanding to take his total length and girth.

*Incredible.*

Zach's breath was hot and heavy, his body not moving. Kat knew he was struggling for control. But she didn't want him controlled. Right now she needed him to feel as earthy and animalistic as she did.

Her hands slipped to his ass, urging him to move. "Please, Zach. I need you."

He pulled back and buried himself again…and again. His fiery demon eyes were completely untamed as he began to pump into her fiercely, her hips meeting his with equal need.

Zach seemed to know exactly what angle, what movements would set Kat aflame. Her heart was racing as he buried his hands into her hair. Right before his lips met hers, she heard him growl, "Mine. You'll always be mine."

His tongue slid into her open mouth with a sense of ownership that took her breath away. He was hungry and greedy, his cock pumping and his tongue invading her mouth.

Kat trembled as she felt her orgasm building. Her fingers bit into his back as she moaned, his mouth swallowing her sounds of pleasure as though he wanted to take them inside himself and savor them.

He broke off the embrace and trailed his tongue along the side of her neck, nipping her earlobe as his hips pistoned his cock in and out of her, over and over.

"Come for me, Kat. I want to feel you climax around me," his deep voice demanded.

He reared up and grasped her hips, burying himself deep and hard. Kat's climax blasted through her. "Oh, God. Yes, Zach. Yes."

Zach continued slamming into her as her channel clutched his cock like a tight fist, spasming over it and flooding it with her thick, creamy fluid.

Kat heard him cry out as her body flew apart, her squeezing spasms triggering his own orgasm. Her back arched as he buried himself inside her, pulling her hips tight against his while he poured himself deep into her womb with a harsh groan.

Her body was still shaking as he rolled to her side, pulling her tightly against him.

"Mine," he choked out, his voice heavy with possession.

Kat's racing heart jumped, secretly thrilled at his verbal branding. She sighed and rested her head against his shoulder.

Neither of them spoke, and there was only the sound of both of them panting as they recovered, the tilting, spinning world finally righting itself.

Several minutes later, Kat remembered why she had sought him out last evening in the den. "Zach…my business account seems to have grown…substantially. Would you happen to have anything to do with it?" She pulled back to look at his face. His expression was solemn, but his eyes were dancing with mischief. She knew damn well that he knew why.

"Consider it a bonus for the excellent job you do in my building."

Exasperated, she shot back, "I water your plants, Zach. I'm not a top executive. Besides…you didn't even know who I was a few days ago."

"I know our plants look fantastic." He gave her a pained look as he saw her disapproving face. "What? You can't take a bonus from a client?"

"You don't give your plant lady a quarter of a million dollar bonus," she answered in an annoyed tone.

"I knew you were worried about money because you aren't making an income this week," he answered honestly. "I didn't want you to be worried."

*Income for the week?* Hell…she wouldn't have to worry about income for years. "You need to take it back, Zach. Reverse whatever you did and take it out of my account."

"No," he answered simply.

Damn. Stubborn. Demon. "Fine, I'll call the bank myself and have it reversed."

"You can't."

Kat sat up and pulled the sheet across her breasts, glaring at him as he moved to lounge against the headboard, his fingers locked behind his head. He flashed her a wicked grin that shot straight to her core.

"Why can't I? It's my account." *Stay angry. Stay angry.* Shit…it was so hard to assert herself when he was splayed out like every woman's fantasy, shooting her that come-take-me-baby look.

He shrugged. "Demon magic. It will go right back into your account again."

"I'm not keeping your money, Zachary Winston." She really was annoyed.

"It's just money, Kat. I don't understand why you're upset." He was giving her a look of genuine bewilderment now.

*Oh, God. He really doesn't understand.* She could tell by the confused look on his face that he didn't have a clue why she was angry. Money didn't mean the same to him as it did to her. He didn't comprehend why she couldn't just take it, why her pride demanded that she had to give back something she hadn't earned. Taking a deep breath, she asked him slowly, "Zach…do you remember what it was like to be poor?"

As Zach's face turned dark and brooding, Kat was almost sorry she had asked the question. She knew it brought back bad memories of his life before he became a Sentinel, before he made the bargain to become a demon. It was a while before he spoke. "I remember. I would have given anything to be wealthy to help Sophie. Unfortunately…I made the wrong wish."

"You bartered your life for that wealth, Zach. I can't take money for doing nothing. I already get paid for the work I do in your building."

One of his previous statements that he had made suddenly popped into her mind as she continued, "Didn't you say that demons can't change a human disease process? That they don't have the power of life and death over human diseases?"

"Yes."

"Then how could you have made another wish that would have made a difference for Sophie?" Kat looked at his tormented face, any annoyance she'd been feeling instantly replaced by compassion. She knew how he felt about making the wrong wish for his sister, but had he been blaming himself for two hundred years for nothing?

"There had to have been something else I could have wished for... something that would have made a difference." Zach's face showed the agony of his struggle and she decided that after two hundred years, it was time for him to let go of it.

Kat grasped both sides of Zach's head, forcing him to look into her eyes. As she stroked his cheek, she told him softly, "It was out of your hands, Zach. There was nothing you could do. You made the right decision. It's time to stop blaming yourself for something that was out of your control."

His face fell and his head dropped. "She was all I had, Kat. The only family I had left-my baby sister. I'd promised my mom I'd take care of her...but I couldn't save her. I was supposed to be protecting her. She was just a kid. " His voice was rough, vibrating with emotion.

Kat's heart melted. He'd loved Sophie fiercely, and she understood his sense of loss. Not only had he lost his young sister, but his reason for existing. He felt the same way she had been feeling since her purpose in life had suddenly come to an end when Nora had gotten married. But she still *had* Nora and Stevie. Zach had lost everything when his sister had died and she had a feeling he had never fully recovered. He was a man who had everything...except love. "How old were you?"

"Seventeen," he answered huskily.

*My God.* He had still been a boy...or at least at the stage where he was caught between being a boy and a man. She hadn't realized he'd been so young. Zach had told her that he was immortal and he obviously had stopped aging by the time he hit thirty or so. She had just assumed that he had been that same age when he had made his demon bargain. He had actually become a demon at the age of seventeen, making a brave decision at a very young age that would have terrified any older adult.

Kat leaned over and draped herself over his torso, slipping her arms around his back and laying her head against his chest. "You did the right thing, Zach."

"It's hard to accept that."

"I know. But you know it's the truth."

His arms tightened around her, holding her like an anchor to keep him grounded while his emotions raged. "I suppose I do," he rasped.

"Tell me about her, Zach. What was she like?"

And Zach did. Once he started talking, it was if he couldn't stop. The dam had broken on memories that had been sealed with guilt and they came flooding out in a rush. Happy. Sad. Funny. Every memory he had flowed out of him, one right after the other.

Kat listened, asking an occasional question or throwing in a comment, but mostly she let him purge himself of anger and remorse by remembering his sister. Finally, when his body was more relaxed and he had stopped talking, Kat asked, "So Kristoff really saved your life?"

"He did," Zach admitted. "We left the workhouse and were sent to work at the factory. I guess Sophie and I were lucky to be sent to the same place together, even though it killed me to watch her be worked the way she was there. I swore I'd get us out of there, find a way to support her better and get her a better life. At least we could sneak time together. When she got sick and got thrown into the pest house, I ran away. The place was no more than a barn filled with dying people who got little or no care. She was sick. Really sick. Her whole body was covered in pox and trying to keep her fever down was nearly impossible. But after a while, I thought she was getting better. I wanted to get her some clean things, blankets and the necessities, but I didn't have any money. So I went into the village and tried to steal what I needed."

Kat tightened her arms around him, running her hand up and down his back, her heart breaking for the impoverished young man he had been. She had been poor, but never like that, without food, a place to live, and the basic necessities. "I would have done the same if it was my nephew. I would have done whatever was needed to provide for him," she told him, knowing it was the truth. "You were caught?"

"I was caught, and they were ready to take me away as a thief when Kristoff came out of nowhere, told them I was his brother, and paid the merchant double to keep his mouth shut." Zach released a long, shaky breath before continuing. "I promised to go with him as soon as Sophie was better. I had pockets full of money from making the bargain with him, and assurances of much more later. I left Kristoff in the village and ran back to Sophie. All I could think about was getting back to her, getting her out of that hellhole and to some place clean and nice." His voice broke, and his speech halted suddenly.

Tears flowed freely from Kat's eyes. She closed them and shuddered, her whole body experiencing Zach's pain. "She was gone." It wasn't a question. She already knew what had happened. But experiencing Zach's emotions, feeling his anguish, made her ache for his loss as though it had just happened. He was too lost to block his sorrow and despair at the loss of his sister, but she didn't care. She'd rather feel it, experience it with him. Being close to him was something she craved, and she'd willingly share his sadness with him. It almost felt like she took some of it away by bearing it alongside of him.

"She was gone, the linen taken away. There was just an empty space where she'd been lying when I left. A bunch of the dead had been buried in a mass grave. I never got to say goodbye," Zach rasped, his voice tight.

Kat sat up and looked at his face. She ran her hand along his cheek lightly, the stubble on his jaw abrading her fingers. *This is the pain he carries. The guilt.* "You were nothing more than a child yourself, Zach. You did the best you could. It isn't your fault. You were very brave."

He reached up and entwined her fingers with his, pressing her hand to his face, his expression ravaged. "It was a long time ago, Kat. Don't cry."

It may have happened two centuries ago, but Kat had felt his torment. He'd never really dealt with the loss, so it was like it was happening all over again. "There's no expiration date on grief," she told him quietly. "I just wish I could do something to help."

Smiling weakly, he pulled her back into his arms, hugging her body tightly against him. "You already have. You calm my soul." He sighed heavily and his body relaxed. "I need you so much."

Kat's chest was aching as she sunk her hands into his hair and let herself relax against him, feeling strangely content, knowing with complete certainty that at this very moment in time, she was exactly where she wanted to be. This thing, this incredible connection to Zach was the most intimate and amazing experience she'd had in her entire life.

"How did you end up with Hunter and Drew?" she asked curiously. Zach had told her that the three men weren't blood-related, but she wondered how they had come together.

"Unlucky, I guess," Zach grumbled playfully.

Kat smiled, knowing he really didn't feel that way about his adopted brothers. "You care about them."

"They're a pain in my ass," he answered swiftly before continuing. "I stayed with Kristoff for about ten years until I started actually taking up my Sentinel duties. He said I needed time to grow up."

She didn't need to ask how that had gone over with Zach. She could hear the irritation in his voice. No doubt he had gotten impatient. "And you met your brothers during your growing up time?"

"No. I had all the money and things I wanted, but we didn't actually start posing as wealthy brothers until they were recruited later by Kristoff. Drew came first, about thirty years after I started working as a recruiter. His parents were farmers during the potato famine in Ireland. Hunter arrived soon after. Eventually Kristoff hooked us up as brothers and business partners to explain our wealth. We all wished for the same bargain and it got harder and harder to explain having that much money without a business or a wealthy family. We've been together ever since."

Kat nodded. "I wondered if Drew was Scottish or Irish. I noticed he still has a touch of an accent. I guess you lost your English accent because you came here so young. What about Hunter? Is he always so gruff?"

Zach snorted. "Gruff? He's an asshole. Has been since he became a Sentinel. But he has good reason. He lost his whole family to the Evils.

Drew and I try to contain him, but he's out of control. Breaks every rule he possibly can, although he does it out of hatred of the Evils."

*Oh God. Poor Hunter. No wonder he looks so bitter.* "I wish we could help him," she whispered softly.

Zach rolled, pinning her body beneath his, all his hard, hot flesh suddenly over her, surrounding her in heat. "Keep your distance from Hunter," Zach warned, his face suddenly grim. "He isn't always...safe."

Kat wasn't so sure about that, but she didn't argue. Honestly, Hunter reminded her of a wounded animal, snarling back at the world because he was hurting. Twining her arms around his neck, she met his fierce glower with a fascinated stare. How had his mood turned so quickly from tender to volatile?

"Because I'm a demon, sweetheart," he answered, eyeing her with hot intent. "And you're my woman. My greatest instinct is to shelter you, protect you, and make you mine."

Kat shivered in anticipation. He was all male dominance and hot demon, a combination that was irresistible. The lure of melting into his possessive embrace was too strong. No man had ever wanted to keep her from harm or had cared about her happiness.

"I do," Zach rumbled, his lips swooping down to capture her mouth.

He laid siege, tempting her before she could chastise him for reading her thoughts again, but within moments, lost in his seductive embrace, she no longer cared.

# Chapter Nine

*D*rew Winston paced his plush office at Winston Industries with a pensive expression, gripping the foam cup in his hand so tightly that it nearly burst. "Do you think he did it?" he asked Kristoff and Hunter, both of whom were currently lounging in his comfortable leather chairs near his desk. They had turned their seats toward the door and were presently watching him walk back and forth across the considerable length of his private office, stopping occasionally to take a slug of his cappuccino or to grab a decadent chocolate from his desk and pop it into his mouth. His personal assistant made sure Drew had an endless supply of both items, and several others that Drew indulged himself with throughout the day. If it were possible for demons to become overweight, Drew was fairly certain he would be. Fortunately, he was immortal, and he never had to worry about what he shoved into his mouth to satisfy his never-ending hunger. His body would always be in optimum fighting condition. There were many things Drew loved about being a Sentinel, and being capable of eating an endless amount of food that wasn't good for him was at the top of the list.

"Which deed are we talking about?" Kristoff questioned with a small, mysterious smile.

"We want to know if Zach bound Kat to him." Hunter turned slightly and tossed his empty soda can toward the trash, the container sailing neatly through the air and landing dead center. "Two points," he grunted with satisfaction.

"He did. Tighter than he realizes," Kristoff replied, a small smile lingering on his lips.

Drew didn't ask how Kristoff knew this. The Sentinel king had powers that even he and his brothers hadn't yet completely figured out. "She accepted him then?" Drew asked, hoping Zach would finally find peace.

"Oh…he hasn't taken her as his *radiant.* She made a life bargain with him," Kristoff commented casually before lifting his own cup of coffee to his mouth, taking a healthy gulp.

Drew's eyebrows drew together, creating a furrow between his brows. "And will he be taking her as his *radiant?*"

Kristoff swallowed before he shrugged and then answered, "That I don't know. No Sentinel has ever *not* accepted their radiant, but if anyone is stubborn enough to do it…it's Zach."

"I'd refuse," Hunter grumbled, crossing his arms in front of him. "Better to not have a mate. Too much trouble."

Drew didn't answer. He was used to Hunter's abrasive personality. And what Hunter was really saying was that it hurt too much to care about someone, to risk losing them. With Hunter's past, it was understandable. He just wished his brother would stop divesting the Evils of their heads without provocation and breaking the rules. Drew hated seeing the price that Hunter paid for doing so, and unfortunately, it happened way too frequently.

"He needs her," he told Kristoff fiercely, gripping his cup until the foam indented and was in danger of popping. Zach deserved his happiness and Kat was his only hope of finding it.

"That may be true, but it's ultimately up to Zach to figure it out. We can't interfere."

*Bullshit. There had to be a way to nudge Zach. Or knock him over the head with a sledgehammer.*

"Leave it alone, Drew. Everything will work out as it's meant to be," Kristoff told him, his voice holding a thinly veiled warning.

"I thought you didn't know whether or not Zach would take Kat as his *radiant*," Drew retorted in an irritated voice as he stopped at his desk for another chocolate, pinning Kristoff with a questioning look as he popped it into his mouth.

"I don't know exactly what will happen. But you can't mess with his destiny," Kristoff cautioned before changing the subject. "What of the Sentinels? Have you heard about any of them having similar dreams?"

Hunter merely shook his head. Drew answered grimly, "No. But it will take time to check with all of them in the area."

They had Sentinels worldwide and although the population wasn't enormous, it would take more than a day for word to travel to all of them.

"I've contacted all of the regional leaders. But they'll need to track down and speak with our people of every designation," Kristoff said impatiently. "How many have been taken so far?"

"Twenty that have been reported. All from various regions of the US. It's hard to know where the little assholes will pop up next," Drew replied, gritting his teeth as he said it. His duty was to protect human life, the instinct deep-seated, and he had failed to protect those who were taken. "There could be some missing who we don't know about yet."

They had guardian Sentinels who checked on all previous rescues occasionally, and they'd never had reason to check more often, not to mention the fact that they just didn't have enough guardians.

"Let's hope not," Kristoff replied, rising as he spoke, conjuring a folder and handing it to Hunter. "Your next assignment. The information is all there. Try to behave yourself this time. Kill when you're provoked. Wait until they give you reason."

Hunter grasped the folder, opened it and placed his hand over the information, absorbing it before replying gruffly, "The assholes provoke me just by existing." Without another word, he teleported out of the office silently, his vitriolic words still vibrating through the room.

"How many times is he going to have to suffer the penalties before he stops?" Drew asked Kristoff, frustrated that Hunter didn't seem to care how many times he got the crap beat out of him and then paid the consequences after the beating.

"It's been nearly two hundred years. My guess is that he will continue to do so until he has a reason to stop," Kristoff said, strangely unconcerned about Hunter's behavior. "Eventually, it will stop."

Honestly, his king was probably correct. No amount of reasoning or penalty had stopped Hunter in the last two centuries. He and Zach had tried for years to get Hunter to temper his actions, but it hadn't worked. How would it stop?

Drew opened his mouth to question Kristoff, but before he could ask, the Sentinel king manifested another folder and handed it to Drew as he informed him, "This is a different type of assignment. One that requires a bit of research."

"What is it?" Drew asked curiously, opening the file only to find no photos, only notes and what looked like copies of emails.

"Apparently, someone is compiling a Sentinel history. A human poking around for information to write a damn book. I need you to find him and stop him. The last thing we need is any information floating around in the human population about us. I don't know how we were initially discovered, and I doubt he's finding many people who are willing to talk, but it could breach our security and the security of all Sentinels. He needs to be stopped and we need to do damage control," Kristoff finished in a disgusted voice.

It wasn't Drew's normal type of assignment, but he understood the importance of finding the source and of the danger of possible discovery. "I'll find him and shut him up."

Kristoff nodded once, abruptly and regally, acknowledging that he knew that Drew would handle it.

Drew disappeared with the file in hand, leaving Kristoff alone in the plush office, a small, knowing smile appearing on the king's lips the moment that Drew vanished.

Kat had lived in Seattle all her life, but she'd seen more of the sights with Zach in the last several days than she had in her entire twenty-seven years in the city. Most of her life had been spent working, going from place to place and never really seeing the beauty surrounding her. She and Zach had been everywhere from the Space Needle, to the lovely beaches, and some of the most exclusive shopping venues in the city. Those outings had taught her just how hard it was to argue with a demon. The more she protested, the more Zach purchased for her. Annoyed, she had finally refused to shop with him. There was very little he *hadn't* bought her and it wasn't really comfortable for her to have him spending money to buy her things. She wasn't used to it.

*Get used to it*. Kat could still hear Zach grumbling those words, and he used the expression frequently.

Now, here she was, primped and wearing an expensive jade-green dress that she never would have bought herself, looking better than she had ever looked in her entire life. And she was on the arm of the hottest man on the planet, ready to enter one of the most expensive restaurants in the city. Zach had been more than willing to transport them to the eatery with his magic, but after the Space Needle incident and her first trip to his home by that method, she had been more than a little wary and had asked if they could please drive. No matter how careful Zach was, she wasn't used to traveling at warp speed. She'd been dizzy and nauseated when they had reached the top of the Space Needle, although they'd had the entire place to themselves as he'd done it late in the evening, after the observation deck had closed, and they had been able to enjoy the view at their leisure.

The evening had been absolutely…magical.

Zach had become more and more relaxed over the last several days, more willing to open up and talk. Still, he was a mixture of tender and possessive, sweet and dominant, and everything about him drew her to him like a magnet. She might be his *radiant*, but Kat knew that she had fallen completely under *his* spell.

*How am I going to forget him after our week is over?*

Kat tried to forget that their days together were numbered and to enjoy just being with Zach. He hadn't made love to her since he'd broken down and talked about his sister, and he hadn't spoken of bonding with her and making her his mate. They had spent the days talking, enjoying each other's company, but they went to bed separately. He probably still read her thoughts occasionally, but she wasn't so sure she even minded that anymore.

The valet attendant had helped her from the car, taking her hand for a brief moment, a polite gesture of assistance, but Kat could swear she had heard Zach growl, and he had reached the other side of the car and divested her hand from the young attendant's with more force than necessary, faster than she could blink.

"Did I actually hear you growl at that man?" she asked as she took a firm grasp on his arm to steady herself in her ridiculously high heels.

"I don't like any man touching you. Can't help it," he rumbled as he guided her up the steps to the restaurant.

Zach sounded like an unhappy child, and Kat smiled as he led her into the opulent lobby of a high-rise building that housed a restaurant she had only ever heard about, but had never imagined she would be eating in. Approaching the elevator, she punched the button indicated on the classy restaurant sign, turning to Zach as she felt his muscles tense beneath her fingers. Concerned, she looked up at him. His jaw was clenched and he looked like a man about to attend his own execution. "Are you okay, Zach?" she asked, worried about his expression and tense body. Something wasn't right. Not only was his body language impossible to mistake, but Kat could sense his unease, and she had never really seen him uncomfortable with his surroundings.

"Don't like enclosed spaces," he told her quietly, his tone revealing his discomfort.

The elevator dinged and Kat hesitated. "I'll go and you can transport yourself up there." A claustrophobic demon? It might have been amusing had she not been staring at Zach's face and his stark expression.

"No. I'm not leaving you," he replied in a husky voice, taking her arm and bringing her into the elevator with him. Punching the button, he leaned back against the wall of the small compartment, trying, but not succeeding, to look nonchalant.

God, how Kat hated seeing Zach vulnerable in this way. "Go. I'll meet you. It's silly to be uncomfortable when you can meet me upstairs.

I've lived in Seattle my whole life, Zach. I can ride the elevator alone," she told him as the elevator lurched and started its slow climb upward.

"No," he ground out between clenched teeth. "You don't need to be alone. You're with me."

Damn. Stubborn. Demon. He was doing this for her, staying with her because she wasn't used to being transported demon style. And although the gesture was very sweet, she hated it. She didn't want him suffering because of her. Moving closer to him, grateful they were the only two in the elevator, she wound her arms around his neck and leaned her body into his, rubbing sensually against his immaculate, expensive gray suit and tie. Nipping at his clenched jawline, she breathed him in, her core flooding with heat at his carnal, masculine scent. "Kiss me," she whispered softly as she reached his ear with her lips, flicking her tongue out to touch his earlobe.

In less than a heartbeat, he switched positions, crowding her against the wall of the elevator, his heated body holding her prisoner and his hands moving, one to the nape of her neck to draw her mouth to his, and the other behind her back, tugging her body into his, getting them as close as they could be without being completely naked.

She moaned into his mouth as his demanding kiss started out as he meant to continue: dominating, hot, and completely consuming. He plundered ruthlessly, and Kat opened to him, surrendering with a slight whimper, her need to get closer to Zach almost painful.

*I need you, Kat. I need you. I wanted to get to know you, but I've missed this.*

It was as if the floodgates of Zach's mind were bursting open and every thought he had was echoing in her brain. Her body burned and her core flooded with incendiary heat as every molecule in her body begged for his possession, longing to be joined to him in every possible way.

Kat came away panting from the torrid embrace, her heart thundering as Zach pulled his mouth from hers, leaving his arms around her for support.

The elevator had stopped and the doors slid open with a smooth, nearly soundless glide, and she let Zach lead her out the confining space, her body and mind still stunned. What had started out as a diversion for Zach had ended up rocking her world. She should have known better. She couldn't be near him without being intoxicated by his scent, captivated by his presence, and rendered mindless by his kiss. Oh well, at least her intention appeared to have worked. He *had* been distracted during the elevator ride.

"Best elevator ride I've ever had," he replied, his voice naughty and amused.

"Probably the only one," Kat muttered as she looked up at his mischievous grin.

"You're the only one I'd ever do it for," he replied candidly.

"How long have you been claustrophobic?" she asked curiously, wondering why he had such a strange reaction.

"I'm not. Not exactly. It's a Sentinel weakness. One that's used as a penalty for breaking Sentinel rules."

As they reached the enormous oak and glass doors of the restaurant, Kat turned to him, a confused look on her face. "Like prison?"

"Yes. Only the cage is magical and inescapable, and being tightly enclosed is torture for a Sentinel, especially when there's no possibility of escape."

"Have you ever had to go there?" she breathed softly, hoping he had never had to endure that sort of punishment.

"No. But Hunter does quite frequently. He lives by his own set of rules and pays the price," he answered, his voice disgruntled as he pulled on the ornate doors to enter the restaurant, putting a hand on the small of Kat's back to lead her into the eatery.

Kat entered the luxurious restaurant with Zach close behind...and all hell broke loose.

## Chapter Ten

Kat never saw the attack coming. As soon as she entered the restaurant, she was seized from behind and held immobile by a creature she couldn't see, nearly suffocated by the limbs that coiled around her neck and ribs, encompassing her torso. She didn't need to see the creature shackling her to it, her back to its front, to recognize it. All she had to do was breathe, the fetid smell nearly gagging her.

*Evil. Big Evil.*

She struggled, kicking back at the demon that was nearly suffocating her, watching as Zach grappled with many others. He'd manifested a sword, swinging it with a skill that was at odds with his immaculate dress.

*He's so outnumbered. I have to help him.*

Screams from hysterical staff and patrons vibrated through the room, but Kat tried to concentrate, tried not to panic, her only thought to help Zach.

One mighty swing of his sword lopped off the head of one of the Evils, and Kat shuddered as it rolled near her feet. There was no red blood. Instead, the beheaded body oozed black slime, the substance as thick as mud.

*I'm going to try to take out the bastard behind you. Then you need to run. Get as far away from here as possible. Find my brothers. They'll protect you.*

Zach's anxious baritone flowed through Kat's mind, a statement that sounded suspiciously like he didn't expect to make it through this fight. "No!" she said furiously, fighting with all of her strength to get away from the Evil, but it only tightened its grip, pressing harder against her throat until she was seeing stars.

"Agree to a life bargain with me and we will show him mercy." The ghastly voice behind her spoke near her ear.

Kat had been surprised the big Evil hadn't paralyzed her, but he was obviously an ancient and arrogant enough to think she was helpless and weak. She'd give her life for Zach without question. It wasn't possible for her to let him die. However, she wasn't sure mercy meant sparing his life.

*No! Don't do it. The only way your life bargain with me will end is if I die. It's the only way they can take you if you agree. They'll kill me anyway. I need to get you out of here.*

Kat had figured as much, but the knowledge that she could do nothing for Zach infuriated her. For every troll that Zach dispatched, it seemed to Kat that several more appeared. Tears rolled down her cheeks as she watched helplessly as Zach tried to cut a path to her, his eyes fierce and deadly. He was bloodied and injured, the Evils ripping his clothing to shreds, leaving raw, bloody wounds as they laid open Zach's skin with their razor-sharp claws.

Desperate, she wriggled her arms, trying to get her hand and forearm into her bag that was dangling at her waist. Her heart was pounding as she clenched her smartphone, grateful for Zach's overprotective nature. He'd added his brothers' numbers and Kristoff's in case of emergency. The big Evil holding her had loosened his hold around her neck, obviously not worried that a helpless human female was going to get away, breathing heavily in excitement as he watched the battle playing out, waiting for Zach to be killed. Aiming carefully, she kicked back with her foot, hoping it would connect with what should be the creature's groin and slammed a fist backward, hoping to hit his face. She went instantly slack and limp in his grip, gaining precious seconds of freedom as she landed at his feet and the troll hissed in pain.

Her fingers flew, texting a SOS to Kristoff and the name of the restaurant. Seconds was all she had. She had just pressed the Send button when she was hoisted up brutally, wincing as she felt the claws of the Evil biting into her skin.

"You'll pay for that, bitch," he snarled, claws sinking deep enough into her upper arms to puncture her flesh.

Her cell phone dropped to the floor, and she desperately hoped that the message had reached Kristoff. Watching Zach as he fought on, she knew he wouldn't stop until he was dead, but he was weakening, blood saturating his body as he continued to lop off the heads of more incoming Evils.

Terrified screams and the sounds of battle continued to vibrate through the room, the patrons and employees all huddled against the back wall, as far away from the battle as they could possibly get.

*Zach. Transport yourself away. Please. You can't keep at this much longer.* She shoved the thought into his mind with a mental push. She couldn't watch him die trying to protect her. He could easily retreat. Save himself. And they couldn't take her to the demon realm as long as he was alive, right? They might be able to hurt her physically, but they couldn't touch her soul, kill her, or take her away. Zach could take care of his injuries, get more Sentinels and come to her rescue.

A loud, reverberating, low sound pulsated through her mind, the sound of Zach's displeasure at that particular suggestion.

Just as she was about to start pleading with him, one by one, Kristoff, Drew, and Hunter appeared in the room, taking instant measure of the situation and joining the fray.

A sob of relief left her lips at the same instant that she felt the Evil dig his claws deeply into her upper arms. Almost instantly, she began to quiver, white-hot pain lancing through her body, an agony unlike anything she had ever experienced before. Her vision started to blur and she could feel perspiration dripping from her skin. She blinked, trying to clear her vision. She could see that the Evils were retreating and her heart leapt with joy, even as her body was consumed in pain.

*Zach won't die. He'll live.*

Her brain flooded with relief as her body burned with excruciating pain before the whole world went dark.

*Dammit! Why didn't she run when she had the chance?*

Zach's whole body quaked with fury as he watched Kat thrashing on his bed, her body covered in a pair of flannel pajamas he'd conjured for her, completely buried under a mountain of blankets. Still she shivered and moaned, her body racked by the pain coursing through every cell in her body.

"Fuck. She should have run like hell when she got away instead of trying to text the three of you," he said huskily, unable to keep his turbulent emotions buried. "The bastard must have injected her with toxins before he disappeared."

Sentinels were immune to that particular weapon in the arsenal of torture devices the Evils utilized. Unfortunately, humans were not, and there was nothing an Evil loved more than releasing the poisons from its claws into a human body and watching its victim suffer.

"She'll live, although the next day or two will be painful for her," Kristoff grumbled, standing at Zach's side with a remorseful expression. "The Evils are getting bolder, blatantly breaking more rules. If Goran could have taken her, he would have. So obviously, there are some things that they still aren't capable of doing, like ignoring your life bargain with her. They couldn't take her because you're still alive. He hurt her just because he could. They can't draw power from a human unless they're in their own realm."

Tearing his eyes from Kat, Zach shot Kristoff a dark look. "Why? Why her? Cut the bullshit and tell me why they're so eager to get to Kat. I know you know. You said she was special. She's my mate. I deserve to know why. I can't fucking protect her if I don't know everything."

Kristoff crossed his arms in front of him, returning Zach's stare. "You'd protect her best by taking her as your *radiant*. Bind her to you.

But you're obviously not ready to do that. The Evils have reason to want *her* in addition to the purity of her soul. She is dangerous to them, and they obviously know it or they wouldn't be gunning for her so hard."

Zach cocked his head, nearly wanting to laugh at Kristoff's comment. His sweet, gentle Kat was dangerous to the Evils?

*Impossible.*

"She couldn't hurt any living thing even if she wanted to," Zach replied, giving his king a skeptical look. "She's not capable of it."

Zach heard his brothers' low murmur of agreement, both of them standing behind Kristoff, listening intently. Since Kat had saved his life with her rash actions, she obviously had the total support of all the Winstons.

"She doesn't have to be anything other than what she is for them to want her. It's her dormant *radiant* abilities they're afraid of," Kristoff replied, running a frustrated hand through his blond locks.

Every *radiant* had a dormant power that was released upon her joining with her Sentinel mate, a benefit that rippled to every one of them in the entire population. That constant infusion of power was one of the reasons the Sentinels had thrived. Rarely was it anything other than a small addition to every Sentinel's magic, a tiny surge felt by every one of them when a joining took place. It was a common occurrence, and Zach rarely even noticed the addition to his powers anymore. "Why is Kat different from any other?" Zach asked, grinding his teeth with impatience. Kat was in pain, suffering, and he fucking wanted to know why.

"She holds the power of realm-walking," Kristoff answered grimly.

Zach looked at Kristoff in horror, hearing a low whistle from his brothers behind the king.

"That's no little burst of power. Sounds more like an atomic bomb," Drew commented, his voice incredulous. "How can she hold that type of magic?"

"Somewhere in her very distant ancestry, one of her descendants was probably a demigod, a child born of a union between one of the gods and a human. The gift is dormant and harmless, passed from generation to generation, and it won't awaken unless she mates with a Sentinel,"

Kristoff said distractedly, as though he were still working through some of the details himself.

"How do you know this?" Zach asked heatedly, his fists clenching in irritation. "And why the hell didn't you tell me?"

Kristoff sighed. "I knew she held special power. I could sense it. But I didn't know what it was until today, when I saw that it was Goran in control of her. I heard his thoughts, his reasons for needing her under their control. I haven't come face to face with Goran in centuries. I learned much from him today."

Zach knew that Kristoff could read his Sentinels, but he'd had no idea that his king could also read the Evils. It made sense in a strange sort of way. Kristoff *was* the Sentinel demon king, and many of his powers were still a mystery, even to the Sentinels closest to him. There were a lot of things that Kristoff didn't explain, and didn't share.

"We could finally enter the demon realm, plan attacks, hurt the assholes really bad." Hunter sounded almost uncharacteristically gleeful.

Kristoff held up his hand in warning. "Hold on. What happens is Zach's decision. This is a decision for eternity for him. If he doesn't want to take Kat as his mate, no one will force him. Our past rescues who have disappeared are already dead, captured with no more than an illusionary trick in the dream realm, a skill that the Evils have obviously mastered. I read the information from Goran. We need to master that same skill and be on guard for it now. What happens with Kat is completely up to Zach."

Zach sat on the bed and threaded his hands through Kat's hair, his chest aching from watching her suffering. "It isn't that I don't want her," he said hoarsely. "I think I want her too much. She deserves better than me, more than a life lived in darkness."

"Did it ever occur to you that you're exactly what she needs?" Kristoff questioned quietly. "Kat's given her whole life for others. More than likely she'll continue to do the same. Who will treasure her more than you? A *radiant* is more than a randomly selected female. She's your match, and you are hers. Do you really want her with a man who won't make her happy?"

*Mine.*

The thought of Kat being with any other male but him made him nearly feral.

Kristoff continued quietly, "Comfort her for now. Your biggest problem in not releasing her *radiant* power is that if you don't, the Evils will never stop pursuing her. But you can decide later. Call if you need us."

Zach could feel the faint stir in the air as his brothers and Kristoff disappeared, but he didn't turn around, didn't take his eyes off his woman.

Normally, he tried to do things the human way to maintain the guise of being normal, but he didn't have the patience at the moment. Zach dissolved his clothing with his magic, his gaze never leaving Kat as he crawled onto the bed and under the covers with her, pulling her trembling body gently against him, her back to his front. Wishing he could absorb her pain, take it into his own body, he curled one arm around her waist, letting the other slip through her hair and buried his face within the silky locks, shuddering as he inhaled her scent.

"I'm sorry, Kat. So sorry," he whispered hoarsely against her ear, wishing he could give her something, anything to ease her pain. Human narcotics would be useless against Evil magic. "This shouldn't have happened to you. None of it. You never should have come into contact with my world."

*Then I would never have met you.*

Startled at hearing her thoughts, Zach lifted his head to see her face, but her eyes were closed. Her body had quieted, leaving only a grimace on her beautiful face that told him she was still hurting. "And that would have been a bad thing?" he asked quietly, his arm wrapping a little more snugly around her body.

*Yes.*

Her answer came so swiftly that it had Zach's heart thundering against the wall of his chest. "How bad is the pain?" he asked anxiously, relieved that she was at least communicating.

*Feels like someone doused me in gasoline and lit a torch. But it isn't so bad now that you're here. What happened?*

Had Zach known that being near her would make her feel better, he would have had no hesitation in booting everyone out immediately and cuddling beside her. Honestly, he'd been afraid his body against hers would make her hurt worse. "The king of the Evils injected you with some toxins before he disappeared. It will go away, probably by morning, but I know it hurts like hell, sweetheart."

*You were hurt. Are you okay?*

The concern and anxiety in her question warmed him. He'd taken some slashes, the amount of blood he'd lost probably making it look worse than it really was. "I'm fine. I'll heal by morning."

*Are you sure?*

Zach smiled against her hair. "I'm positive. I'm worried about you. You should have run when you had the chance."

*I'd never leave you and run away to save myself. You needed help.*

Zach's smile broadened as he absently twisted one of her wayward locks of hair that reminded him of the sun around his finger. "But you wanted me to go and leave you? And just so you know…that would never happen," he told her roughly, his throat clogged with emotion.

*I was scared. I didn't want anything to happen to you.*

"I'm immortal, Kitten. Very few things other than losing my head, literally, are going to kill me. The same doesn't apply to you. You should have run," he muttered, slightly disgruntled, but touched by the way she cared about him.

Kat's entire essence seduced him, ensnared him as no other ever had, and he was helplessly torn between his need to make her his, and his need to provide her with a better life, a happier life than she would probably have with him.

Now, she would have very little choice. To stay safe, she would need to become his *radiant,* releasing her power, and taking away any further reason for the Evils to have any interest in her. If she didn't, they would pursue her to the ends of the earth. Hell, he could certainly provide her with a better life than constantly being on the run from Evil demons.

*I'll protect her. Shelter her. She'll be my radiant and I'll make her happy. I'll make it up to her, give her everything she needs and wants.*

Zach didn't trust anyone with Kat's safety anymore except himself. His need for her was too great, his attachment to her too immense, his drive to protect her too damn strong. In the span of six short days, the woman in his arms had become everything to him.

He didn't give a shit what sort of dormant magic she held inside her; all he cared about was her, making her his, binding them together.

Kat's breathing was deep and even, causing Zach to release a masculine sigh of relief. At least she was sleeping restfully, finally free from the pain of the toxin.

Closing his eyes, he tried to relax his body and sleep, but all he could think about was that damn bargain, and he cursed himself for ever making it. He didn't want Kat under demon compulsions. He just wanted…her.

Pulling her tightly against him, he felt her warmth seeping into his soul, as he had felt it for every hour of every day they'd been together.

*I'm a lucky bastard to have her for a mate. I don't deserve her.*

Unfortunately, he couldn't help but feel that she was getting the short end of the deal. But, like it or not, she would be his. Her life depended on it now.

*I can make her my radiant and still set her free to live a better life. She doesn't have to stay with me or live in my world.*

Even as the thought rolled through his mind, Zach felt a growl rise up in his throat. To let Kat go after he released her power would be nearly impossible. Sentinels may have evolved and become nearly human, but his core was still…demon. And his demon need for Kat was completely animalistic and elemental. Yet, his desire for her to be happy struggled against those primitive desires. She'd spent her adult life catering to the needs of others.

*Because she has such a huge capacity to give and sacrifice for those she loves.* Christ. He'd give anything to be a recipient of that kind of love. He'd been alone so long, so fucking lonely. These days with Kat had been the first time he'd ever really felt alive and whole in two centuries.

His mind troubled and weary, it was quite some time before Zach finally fell into a restless sleep.

# Chapter Eleven

"You want me to be your mate?" Kat looked at Zach, turning away from the cup of coffee she had been doctoring with cream and sugar, to make sure she had heard him properly. She'd been out like a light all night and most of the day, sleeping off the effects of the Evil's poison. Maybe she wasn't hearing him properly, or her brain wasn't quite processing his words right. After she had showered and come downstairs to make something for dinner, she had felt okay. She and Zach had made sandwiches and had eaten together, talking mostly about the horrors of last night. She had thought she was pretty much back to normal. Now...she was starting to doubt she was totally functional.

*It's not possible that he wants to bind himself to me for eternity.*

Problem was, he looked completely serious, and as her gaze raked over him, as he leaned that hot, muscular body against the opposite wall of the kitchen, she knew she *had* heard correctly. He nodded slowly, his hungry eyes meeting her startled gaze with a stare so intense it sent shivers down her spine.

Picking up her coffee mug, she asked him casually, "Why?" He hadn't ever mentioned her bonding with him before, or the two of them mating.

Pushing himself off the wall, he stalked toward her slowly, his thumbs in the pockets of his jeans, his eyes molten. "Is it really so hard to believe that I want you?"

*Um…honestly…yeah. It is hard to believe.*

Kat didn't answer aloud. She raised her coffee to her mouth and took a sip, watching him move slowly toward her.

He got as close to her as he possibly could without touching her, crowding his large body next to hers, leaning one hip against the cupboard. "I think we've had this discussion before, Kitten. I don't want to be without you," he replied huskily, his eyes never leaving hers. "But there are certain things that you need to know. You deserve better than me. I know that. But nobody will ever cherish you as much as I will, if you just say yes."

Kat released a shaky breath that she hadn't realized she had been holding. She had never known it was possible for a man to look both incredibly dominant and vulnerable at the same time. But Zach definitely did. His face expressed a variety of emotions, unguarded and raw, and it made her heart ache. "What do we have to do? Are you sure that's what you want?"

"I know exactly what I want. I'm looking at her right in front of me. It isn't a question of what I want. This is about you," he grumbled, taking the mug from her hand and setting it on the counter so he could match her palm to his. "If we bond, some of the lightness of your soul will transfer to me and you will receive a small piece of my darkness inside you. It won't change who you are, but you'll carry a small piece of my dimmer soul with you forever. Personally, I think it's fucked up, but that's the way the Sentinel bonding works." Entwining their fingers, he took their joined hands and laid them gently on his chest.

Honestly, there wasn't anything Kat wanted more than to give Zach some light in his life. He certainly hadn't had any throughout his demon existence, spending most of that time feeling guilty about the decisions he had made when he was little more than a child. And carrying a small piece of his soul actually was appealing. In fact, she craved it. If Zach was darkness, she'd willingly wallow in it. He might think his soul was completely black, but Kat knew it wasn't. "I want it. I want you." Her words were a whisper filled with longing, the only thing she was able to say.

His eyes starting to glow, he trapped her against the counter, his expression fierce. "This is forever, Kat."

Oh yeah, she could definitely do eternity. If Zach would look at her like this forever, want her this way for the rest of their existence, she'd never be lonely again. But she'd get old while he...wouldn't.

"You won't age after we bond. Our life forces will be bound," Zach answered, obviously reading her thoughts. "Our demon bargain is over. It ended at sunset. I can't tell you how fucking happy I am that we can do this without the influence of the compulsions."

How could she explain that she'd always known the difference between the compulsions and her own emotions? She'd wanted Zach desperately almost from the moment she had met him, and she knew her feelings weren't the result of the demon bargain. "Nora and Stevie?" What would happen with them?

"You'll never be able to tell them. For a while, they'll see you age appropriately as they do, but at some point you'll have to fade out of their life and the lives of their descendants." Zach looked pensive and nervous, the muscles in his biceps rippling as his whole body tensed. "Hell...there's nothing about the arrangement that's fair and I know you're getting a raw deal, but I still want you to say yes. I need you to say yes. I'm a demon, I'm selfish, and I want you to agree more than anything I've ever wanted in my entire existence," Zach told her in a low baritone vibrating with emotion. "I'm doubtful I can even give you a child of your own. Children between a Sentinel and a *radiant* are rare."

Kat hesitated, even though she knew exactly what she wanted. It was habit, a moment of lingering doubt that a man like Zach was ready to make an eternal commitment to a woman like her. But he had just told her how he felt, and she believed him. She had practically raised Stevie with Nora, and she didn't feel the desperate need for a child of her own. But she did crave Zach. If she wanted happiness, if she wanted to reach out and take something she desperately wanted just for herself, all she had to do was say it. "There's no guarantee any couple can have a child, and if we can't, I'm okay with that. So, yes. Please. I want to be your mate, Zach."

He was on her before she had a chance to breathe, seizing her around the waist and transporting them to his bedroom.

He did the transfer slowly, and she ignored the slight dizziness as she looked up at Zach's heated eyes, his look dark and fierce as he stripped naked, his hot, possessive gaze never leaving hers.

"Once I speak the words, I'll be bound and helpless, Kat." His voice was husky and filled with yearning. He reached for the tie on the silken robe she had donned upon waking, groaning as he found her body naked beneath it, her gown dropping to the floor without a sound. "I'll be powerless until you accept me."

Kat knew the basics. Zach had explained how a Sentinel mating worked in general terms, and it had conjured erotic images that she'd never be able to forget.

He turned and ripped back the top sheet and the quilt, leaving only the bottom silk sheet. It was a soft, creamy white that contrasted with his dark body as he lay down in the center of the bed, waiting for her.

Her hands were trembling as she crawled onto the bed, humbled beyond words that he trusted her enough to be completely vulnerable to her. "Won't this be difficult for you? You don't like being confined," she murmured softly as she knelt beside his body.

Mates had to come to a Sentinel of their own free will, the demon willingly and magically bound to ensure that the union was the *radiant's* choice.

She would have total control of this fierce, spectacular man/demon. The thought was heady and so erotic that she could barely contain her longing to touch him.

"No. If every moment of it brings me closer to having you as my mate, I won't even notice," he answered her question hoarsely. He uttered a few lyrical words, a harsh demand in the ancient Sentinel language that would start binding them together for eternity.

When he finished, Kat looked at her demon, helpless and at her mercy, his arms at his side, unable to do much more than strain against invisible bindings. Tears rolled from her eyes, knowing how difficult this was for him, even though he denied it.

"Take me, Kat. Dear God, please touch me." His plea came out as a strangled groan that set her into motion. If he was willing to do this for her, she was determined to make it extremely pleasurable for him.

Kat straddled him, her hands running over his rippling muscles on his chest. He was hers. This incredible, infuriating, hot, sexy male was all hers.

"Mine," she whispered, fierce possessiveness overwhelming her senses as she joined their lips together in a kiss that made her toes curl. She might be in control, but his tongue mastered hers, entwining them with a passion that stole her breath. He devoured her mouth as she threaded her fingers in his hair and rocked her quivering wet mound into his belly in a slow, sliding motion.

Zach panted as his mouth broke away from hers, his expression wild and untamed. It unleashed an answering feral desire in her that was so intense she nearly climaxed as her clit slid against the firm muscles of his abdomen.

"Ride me, Kat." She smiled at his demanding tone as he tugged against his bonds.

"Who's in charge right now, demon?" She knew she'd never have this chance again. Zach was definitely, unashamedly, an alpha male and it thrilled her sexually. But this was a novelty that was so erotic and hot that she couldn't resist playing with him, trying to pleasure him.

He growled as she slid down his body, gently biting at his nipples, flicking them with her tongue as her hands caressed every inch of his burning skin.

"You're playing with fire, Kitten." He snarled the warning, making her shiver, but not with fear. Adrenaline coursed through her body, his out of control wildness sweeping over her, making her desperate to satisfy him.

Kat kissed and licked her way down until she could grasp his rock hard member in her hand. She gripped him firmly, dying to taste him, hungry for his essence. She moaned as she licked the slippery drop at the head. He tasted like Zach...and his flavor was addictive. She could feel him jerking against the binding as she slid her lips over the engorged shaft, grinding her mound against his leg.

His hips rose off the bed with a power that lifted her body as he fought to thrust into her mouth. "Fuck. Ride me, Kat. Now."

Her body was burning for him as she moved her lips slowly and sensually along his cock, loving the feel of the huge shaft between her lips. Her cheeks bulged and hollowed as she sucked him slowly, lost in erotic lust and the unique taste of her mate.

"Kat!" His command was desperate and demanding all at once.

Reluctantly, she removed her lips, wanting to suck him until he released so that she could drown in his ecstasy, but she had to have him inside her. Moving sensually up his body, she shimmied until her pussy was directly above his twitching cock. Her hands braced on his chest, she rolled her hips. Already saturated and aroused nearly beyond endurance, she drenched his cock as it glided along her clit. "Oh, God, you feel so good, Zach."

"Take me inside you. I need to be joined to you. Now." He was demanding, cajoling, his body writhing as though he needed to fuck her or die.

It was one of the hottest things Kat had ever seen.

No longer able to go another moment without him filling her, Kat reached for him, placing the head against her begging entrance. She sank down onto him, her channel opening, stretching as he slid inside her.

His hips strained as he pumped his groin upward, impatient and wanting.

They groaned together as he buried himself to his balls inside her with a hard thrust.

Kat rocked, loving the feel of him filling every inch of her. He consumed her, pouring into every lonely place inside her.

"Fuck me, Kat," Zach demanded, as his hips thrust up again and again, the motion urgent.

Her hips crashed down as his rose, desperate to ride him hard as her need grew so intense that her clit throbbed and her whole body ached for release.

She was lost in the frenzied mating, their bodies coming together forcefully as her hips pumped furiously, taking his cock again and again. Harder and harder.

"Mark me, Kat," Zach growled as he pistoned in and out of her wet heat, thrusting his hips up to meet hers, impaling her with a strength that left her breathless with every thrust.

Seized by an erotic heat that racked her body with tremors, she stretched over him, her breasts sliding along his chest that was slick with sweat. Electric sensation slid down her spine as her hard, hypersensitive nipples brushed against him. Her urge to mark him as her own was so out of control that Kat bit his shoulder with so much animalistic desire that her teeth sunk into his skin deep enough to draw a few drops of blood.

"Oh, Christ. Yes," Zach cried out as he threw his head back and his body tensed.

*Mine.*

Kat pulled her teeth from his skin, watching as the ancient mating mark formed where she had bitten him, her heart pounding with a possessive instinct that slammed through her body.

The second after the mating mark formed, Kat found herself slammed flat on her back, her wild-eyed demon on top of her. His binding had ended as soon as she had marked him.

Zach had flipped them, taking control as he grasped her ass with one hand and cradled her head with the other as he rolled. "Did you enjoy teasing your demon?" His voice was low and dangerous, the question rhetorical.

She spread her legs wide, welcoming his pummeling thrusts as he drove into her with a power he had never used before. She needed it... this total, all-consuming possession. "Yes, Zach. Please." Kat wanted his powerful strokes as he buried himself inside her again and again. "Make me yours."

"You were always mine," he told her tightly, his lips poised against her skin.

She welcomed his ferocious bite when his mouth clamped onto her shoulder, shuddering with the relief of being marked as his mate. Erotic heat infused her, making her burn with a white-hot intensity. "Oh, God, Zach," Kat screamed as she felt the heat of the mark forming.

His mouth left her shoulder and covered hers, owning it with his tongue.

Kat felt invisible hands everywhere. Her nipples were being nipped and stroked, her clit laved by an unseen tongue while she was being furiously taken by her untamed, uncontrollable demon.

He was tormenting *her* now, using his demon magic to make her come apart.

Kat ripped her mouth from his. "It's too much, Zach. Too much." She whimpered as her head rolled from side to side, the intensity of her impending climax more than she could bear.

Her orgasm ripped through her body while Zach continued to show her no mercy.

"Never torment your demon, Kitten. Now all I want is to make you come until you're screaming my name in ecstasy," he whispered roughly in her ear, pinning her hands over her head as she squirmed against him. Their sweat-soaked bodies slid together as Kat panted between orgasms.

Kat wasn't sure where one orgasm stopped and the next began. She climaxed helplessly, writhing and screaming underneath Zach's powerful body as he made her come undone, mindless of anything but her pounding release.

She curled her fingers, digging her nails into his wrists as he held her helpless. She felt him trembling as her pussy gripped and released on his thrusting cock.

"Mine," he groaned as he buried himself inside her while his scorching hot release flooded her clenching channel.

He released her wrists and his demon magic subsided as Kat continued to quiver from her last climax. He gathered her into his arms and rolled to her side. "You're mine, Kat. Forever."

Gasping for air, she couldn't answer. She wrapped herself around him as she sucked oxygen back into her lungs.

She jerked as his thoughts started flowing through her mind.

*I've always missed you, Kat. Always needed you. I just didn't know it until I saw you.*

Zach's voice. Zach's thoughts.

*I need you, too, Zach.*

She answered him without speaking. *Amazing.* They had mental communication, and it was so much more intimate than she had imagined. He had been able to read her thoughts and she had been able to force her words into his mind when she needed to, but now she heard every one of *his* thoughts, felt *his* every emotion, and they flowed into her mind and body as effortlessly as breathing.

"Incredible," she whispered, her body infused with warmth as their thoughts flowed back and forth through an intimate channel.

"I thought this would be the difficult part. My thoughts are dark and yours are light. I didn't want to submerge you in darkness," Zach mumbled aloud, spearing his hand into her hair and kissing her gently on the forehead.

Wrapping her arms around his neck, she snuggled into his warm body, feeling as if everything was exactly as it should be. "It doesn't. It feels perfect."

Exhausted, she closed her eyes, absorbing Zach's essence, an exquisite wholeness she had never experienced before. Relaxed, she started to drift, her body sinking into a contented slumber.

Needing to tell him how she felt before she succumbed, she murmured softly, "I love you, Zach."

Before he could reply, Kat quaked violently, her thoughts suddenly chaotic, as she sunk into a profound and frightening darkness, her body disappearing in front of Zach's anguished eyes.

# Chapter Twelve

"Where in the hell is she?" The shouted question came out as a howl as Zach, his expression tormented, struggled for control.

Zach had appeared in Kristoff's palatial home just moments earlier, desperate and furious, his boots stomping across the marble floor as he went through door after door, seeking his king. Finally, after slamming through the third set of enormous double doors, he found Kristoff seated casually in a huge leather chair, his two brothers occupying the others on each side of his leader.

Zach had to control the urge to throttle Kristoff, his anxiety so high over Kat's disappearance that he was having a very hard time not going completely demon on all of their asses. His mind was clouded over with a rage so black that his control was on a very thin thread that was ready to snap, and his discipline was shot. He was a Sentinel demon worried about his mate, and everything else was thrust into the back of his mind as those ancient instincts consumed him.

Kristoff frowned, his expression troubled as he stared at Zach's face. "What happened?"

"She's gone. Fucking disappeared when she fell asleep. What the hell is happening?" He sounded rash and desperate, but he didn't give a damn. Hell, he *was* desperate. His mate had vanished without a trace, gone in the blink of an eye. One moment he had been holding her warm cuddly body against him, and the next he was in bed alone, his arms empty. "I know you know more than you're telling me, and it's bullshit. She's my *radiant*. My whole damn life now." Zach knew he had never spoken truer words in his entire existence. Kat *was* his life, and he didn't want to even contemplate being without her. And it wasn't just because she was his *radiant*. Yeah, maybe he had tried to bullshit himself about letting her go so she could live a better life, but it wasn't happening. No one cared about her more than he did, and no one ever would. He'd fucking make her happy if it killed him.

Kristoff stood, releasing a heavy sigh. "She's realm-walking. I told you she had that power, Zach."

"*Radiant* power. It should have released to the Sentinels," Hunter said tightly, bringing his muscular body out of the chair to stand beside Kristoff. "But I didn't feel anything."

"I didn't either." Drew stood, his brows drawn together in a contemplative expression.

"The power was released, but not to us," Kristoff stated gruffly. "I never said it would be. The power is hers, an ancient power from a deity. I honestly didn't know exactly what would happen. Now I know. She's the key to other realms, a gatekeeper with a key to enter. Obviously she isn't used to the power. She's wandering."

"She's lost?" Zach whispered huskily, the thought nearly bringing him to his knees. Kat was alone, unprotected, floating from realm to realm. She had to be scared...and he wasn't there with her. "I have to get to her."

Kristoff laid a hand on Zach's shoulder as he said in an eerily sedate voice, "Connect to her. You need to calm yourself and make contact. She's your *radiant* and your mate. You have the connection. You need to focus."

Zach drew in a sharp breath, trying to gain control of the protective, frantic emotions coursing through his body. He *would* get control. Kat's safety depended on it. He'd been so damn out of control when she had disappeared that he hadn't remembered that they had mind contact as mates, an unbreakable connection.

"It won't be easy to link with her in different realms, especially since the connection is new, but you can do it," Kristoff warned, but his voice held encouragement as well. "Concentrate."

Drew moved closer, letting his hand drop to Zach's other shoulder. Hunter moved in and slapped his hand over Drew's. It was a gesture of support, but they were all lending him their magic as well, helping him to calm and focus.

Zach shuddered as their demon magic combined and swirled throughout his body. Closing his eyes, he focused only on Kat-her warmth, her strength-trying to follow her trail. The path was subtle, so weak that he almost missed it. But her essence was as familiar to him as his own now, and he latched onto it, following her course through the dream realm. Her presence got stronger as her path grew darker, carrying him through another vortex, dumping him into a domain so vile that even he recoiled as the stench of evil reached out to him.

*Zach?*

Her voice was weak, frightened, but it was his Kat.

*Don't come here, Zach. Don't. Please.*

"Fuck," he whispered fiercely, finally sealing his connection with his mate.

"Did you find her?" Drew questioned quietly.

"She's in the demon realm. She has no idea what's happening and she can't control her power," Zach answered, pissed off and frustrated as he narrowed in on her exact location.

The moment he pinpointed her position, he could feel her power vibrating throughout her body. He dived into it, using it to bring him to her. For a moment, he wasn't sure it would work, even though she was his mate. Then, his body began to fade, and he fell into a vacuum that sucked him straight to Kat…and directly into demon hell.

Kat shivered even though she was surrounded by flames. She was still naked, and stranded in what she already knew was the demon realm.

She'd already seen Evils of all shape and sizes wandering through the spurts of fire she was trying to avoid. Her stomach lurched as she accidentally took a breath through her nose. *Big mistake.* The stench and squalor all around her stunk, an odor so noxious that it nearly made her heave. Breathing through her mouth was the only way to bear it, and she tried not to think about what was entering her lungs as she gasped for air. She didn't look down as she moved slowly, ducking behind mounds of bones and other refuse that were taller than she was.

*Don't think about what you're walking through or what else is in those piles. Just move.*

Still confused and disoriented, Kat tried to focus on moving forward, getting out of what felt like a nightmare.

*I can't be dreaming. I'm feeling physical pain every time I step on a hot spot.*

Somehow, Kat knew she wasn't dreaming. Zach's connection to her had felt all too real, and she had already floated through the dream realm on the way to this hellhole. And she had recognized it as the dream realm, just as she recognized this as the demon realm.

*What the hell is happening to me?*

Her whole body was vibrating with power, an unsettling feeling as she had no idea what to do with it. If anything, it made her feel all the more helpless.

*Focus. Get out of here.*

She had come through a vortex of some sort. There had to be a way out before she was discovered, and it was only a matter of time. She had avoided detection by ducking behind a mound of rubbish every time an Evil passed by, but eventually, she would be found.

She tried not to think about Zach as she made her way to the next pile of trash. He couldn't come here. Then they would both be trapped.

"I'd rather be trapped with you than live free without you," Zach's low, deep voice whispered into her ear as he slipped his arm around her waist.

Kat nearly squeaked with surprise, but Zach had covered her mouth with his other hand.

*Crap. You nearly gave me heart failure.* Kat spoke to Zach silently, their mental connection solid.

She turned and put her arms around his neck, letting herself be sheltered by his strong body. Tears poured down her face as he tightened his arms around her protectively. She was torn between her relief at seeing him and anger that he had come to her.

"Did you really think I wouldn't?" he rasped into her ear. "Shit. This place is even worse than I imagined. And I don't have any of my powers here."

He let go of her long enough to yank the t-shirt from his jeans and pull it over his head. Lifting her arms, he dropped the garment over her head, covering her nude body. "Not that I wasn't enjoying the view, but I don't think this is the place for me to be distracted by looking at you." He kept his voice low, pulling her back into his arms.

*I don't know how I even got here. Or how to get out.* She clung to Zach, wondering if they were both stuck now.

"We'll get out. This wasn't exactly what I had in mind for a honeymoon destination," Zach grumbled as his eyes scanned the area.

She bit her lip to keep from laughing, feeling safe now that Zach was here. "We aren't married," she reminded him in a hushed voice.

"We're mated. And we will be married," he informed her in an arrogant tone. Grabbing her by the shoulders, he pulled back to look into her eyes. They were glowing amber as he added, "Kat, you have to get out of here. I don't have time to explain, but you have the power to get out. You just need to focus it. Try to center it in your gut and concentrate on where you want to be."

"What about you? I'm not leaving you here." Even if she did have the power, she wasn't going without Zach. Obviously…he didn't have the magic to escape. He had already admitted he was powerless in this realm.

Zach shook her lightly. "Leave. Concentrate. Do it now before we're discovered."

His face was fierce, but Kat could see the underlying concern in his desperate expression. He'd stay and perish just to see her safe. "No. I'll find a way to take us both."

"I'll follow. Just gather your power and get out," he demanded, his expression unyielding.

Kat knew he was lying. She was inside his mind and he wasn't blocking their path of communication.

"She can't. She's stuck here and so are you. Mastering the art of realm-walking takes time and instruction." The voice was deep, casual and yet chastising. "You both need help. If you had stayed long enough, Zach, I would have told you what to do."

Kat turned, her eyes frightened, her knees nearly giving way in relief as she saw a disgruntled Kristoff, his arms crossed in front of him, obviously displeased.

Zach slipped an arm around her waist, pulling her against his body as he answered simply, "She's my mate."

With a small, veiled smile, Kristoff answered, "Glad you finally figured that one out."

Kat was just opening her mouth to whisper a retort when she caught something unexpected, a movement off to her left. Two women were walking together, moving out of an alcove on the other side of the huge room and toward a large door. They were walking away, their back to her, but she had caught their profile as they'd turned, and they were definitely *not* Evils. "Women. Human females," she said, her voice hushed and confused. "They're alive. We have to help them."

"No. We can't. Not now," the Sentinel king answered sternly. Stepping forward, Kristoff laid a hand on each of their shoulders and they all vanished, leaving the dismal surroundings of the demon realm behind.

Zach let fly a very long string of curses as all three of them arrived in his bedroom. Holding Kat tightly against him, he glowered at Kristoff. His first instinct had been to protect his mate; his second to rescue the humans in the demon realm. "You knew," he accused his king. "There are human females still alive in that realm. Why?" The Evils used humans and threw them away once they had served their purpose. As soon as their souls were drained, they no longer needed them.

Removing his hands from Zach and Kat, Kristoff folded his arms across his broad chest, his expression stony as he answered, "They're still useful to the Evils or they would be dead. I was aware that they had prisoners, a few humans with souls that didn't completely drain and re-energized after power was taken from them by the Evils. They are used over and over again by them," Kristoff said sadly, his expression tight.

"Why didn't you tell us? We have to-"

"You can do nothing, Zach. None of us can. It's not time. We don't have the power to rescue them. These are all women who made a demon bargain. I can't pull them from the demon realm. They would pay the penalty of death for breaking their bargain. "

"You're able to transport there?" Zach answered. "Why didn't you tell us that?"

Kristoff let out an audible breath as he answered impatiently, "For what purpose? I'm king. I can go there, but I pay the price for it, and so will you. And we can do nothing. We have no power there and we can't take out prisoners right now. The only reason I could retrieve you and Kat is because you are not under an Evil's bargain."

Even as the Sentinel demon king spoke the words, Zach felt his entire body quake, and his internal organs burn like they had been set on fire with a very large torch. He released Kat and sank onto the bed, staring up at Kristoff, noticing his face was pale. "How do we pay for it?" he asked, afraid he already knew. "Kat?" he rasped as his skin started to burn white hot. Turning his eyes to his mate, she looked alarmed for him, but showed no signs of pain.

"Kat will be well," Kristoff answered. "She's a realm-walker, through a power given to her by a god and released when you were mated. She's now immune to the Evil's toxins in any realm. You and I, however, are not." Sinking into a chair, he continued, "We are protected against toxins on the human plane, but are infected with them the moment we enter the demon realm. If you would have waited, I would have gone to Kat once you located her so we weren't both poisoned."

Zach's jaw was tight as he answered, "Would have gone anyway." He looked up at Kat, her face tormented as she sat beside him and stroked his thigh. "She's worth it." Even as the excruciating pain tore through his entire body like a force of nature, Zach didn't regret going after Kat. And he never would. He'd always go after her.

"You need to lie down," Kat ordered, looking first at him and then at Kristoff.

The Sentinel demon king waved off her concern as he instructed, "Make him comfortable. He's in for a rough ride."

*No shit. I feel like somebody is trying to remove my incinerated internal organs with a dull knife.* Still, Zach tried to close his thoughts, unwilling to have Kat suffer with him.

Two seconds later, Zach found himself flat on his back in bed, his body nude but covered by the sheets and quilt. He knew the change in position was courtesy of his king's magic, but he didn't have time to comment before his entire being was engulfed by a pain unlike anything he'd ever experienced, and he was thrown into the depths of Hell.

# Chapter Thirteen

Kat choked back a sob as she watched Zach thrash with pain, his eyes tightly closed, his face ashen and tormented. Still dressed in only Zach's t-shirt, she crawled into the bed with him, tears rolling down her face as she begged Kristoff, "Please. Tell me what I can do to help him." The king sat stoically in the chair across the room, his own face strained.

"He won't die. But he'll hallucinate and feel so much pain that he might wish he was dead for the next two days," Kristoff answered stiffly.

"I need to help him. Is this the same thing I felt when I was infected by the Evil's claws?" she asked, her voice shaky.

Kristoff shook his head. "It's different. You were injected but the toxins wore off fairly quickly, although I know you were in severe pain. Zach is truly infected. It's more severe, a penalty as well as a poison. The intensity won't stop for two days. It doesn't improve during that time."

"Oh God," Kat moaned, not sure how Zach could withstand that level of pain for two days. "What about you?"

"I'm king. I'm more powerful, and it won't be as severe for me. I've built up a tolerance since I've been to the demon realm before. I'll be fine," he answered, still entirely alert, but not looking very healthy either.

Zach groaned, and Kat flinched, sharing his pain. But even in his tormented state, she could sense him trying to block his thoughts.

Stubborn demon. Wrapping her arms around his body, she tried to shelter him. "I feel so helpless." And she hated it.

"You're his mate, Kat. You can reach him, try to take away some of the anguish. I can guarantee most of his hallucinations will be about you. He'll think you're being harmed or killed. A Sentinel's worst nightmare, not being able to protect the people he cares about," Kristoff commented quietly.

If there was any chance she could ease Zach's pain, she'd do it. He was in this condition because of her, because he'd come after her. "Why did you have to come after me? This is my fault," she whispered softly to Zach, her voice both loving and frustrated.

Kristoff shrugged slightly. "Because he's willing to risk anything for you." Leaning forward, he rested his elbows on his knees, staring intently at Kat. "This isn't your fault, Kat. You had a different kind of dormant *radiant* power, something we've never seen before. What would happen with your magic as a realm-walker was an unknown situation to all of us. Even to me. But no Sentinels go to the demon realm again if we can avoid it. After this next forty-eight hours, you'll understand why. I'll help you control your new ability, but the time hasn't come for us to rescue the human women there. We can't. Not yet. The effort would be futile." He nodded toward Zach as he finished.

"I understand. And I don't want to see anyone else suffer like this. How can I help him? I love him," she answered, desperate. If there was a chance to save Zach some of this torture, she'd do it.

Kristoff smiled slightly, looking satisfied with her answer. "It won't exactly be easy on you."

"I don't care. Tell me."

Kristoff explained patiently before fading away to deal with the fallout from entering the demon realm.

*Focus, dammit. Focus.* Kat had been concentrating on staying in the core of Zach's mind for two straight days, but being constantly bombarded by his torment was almost unbearable. His body was racked with unceasing pain, and the focus of his hallucinations all seemed to be…her. He didn't know what was real or imaginary, so he was experiencing every vision as if it were really occurring. And even though she knew everything he was seeing was an illusion, his pain was all too real. Trying to avoid being caught in the web of false scenes playing in his brain, she tried to watch the current scene of her being tortured and killed by the Evils as though it were a bad movie. *Really bad.*

Her arms wrapped around his groaning, sweaty, and thrashing body, Kat broke through to Zach's consciousness. "Zach. I'm alive. It's just an illusion. I'm here with you," she whispered softly, focusing on the small thread of his rational mind that she was holding onto…just barely.

*Kat? No, you can't be Kat. She's dead.* His internal voice was as agonized and raw as his emotions.

"I'm here. I'm not dead. This will all be over shortly. Please. Hang on and trust me," she begged.

It was a scenario they had been through over and over again in the last two days, and her body was screaming with emotional and physical exhaustion. Zach would calm for a short while and then the agony would start all over again. She'd tried to take some of his physical pain, but found it impossible. He wouldn't release it to her. He might not be conscious, but his damn stubborn nature refused to let her take any of the burning pain that she knew accompanied his mental anguish. Every time she tried, he balked, holding onto his agony instead of letting her share it with him, bring it to a manageable level for him by taking some of it into her body.

*Even in his current state, he's protecting me.*

"Kat!" Zach jackknifed into a sitting position, howling her name like a wolf in torment, his chest heaving as his eyes frantically scanned the dimly lit room.

"Zach? Are you okay?" She sat up, laying a hand on his muscular forearm.

His eyes were glowing, drilling into her like a laser as he jerked his head toward her voice. "Are you really here?" he asked in a husky voice, his eyes brimming with incredulous joy, but wary.

"I'm fine. You were suffering delusions from going to the demon realm. It poisoned you. You've been out for two days now," she answered, running a hand up and down his arm to soothe him.

"Fuck." He ran a hand down his face and through his sweat-dampened hair. "You were there, but I didn't know whether your death was real or if we were together." He lifted her bodily onto his lap and wrapped his arms around her, pulling her against his trembling body. "You stayed with me. Tried to take my pain."

"Yes," she agreed softly, her mouth against his ear as she held him. "But you're so damn bullheaded that you wouldn't share."

"I want to share a lot of things with you, sweetheart, but that kind of pain isn't one of them," he murmured as he tightened his hold, clinging to her like he'd never let her go, fisting large portions of his t-shirt that she was still wearing.

Exhausted, she laid her head on his shoulder. "We both need a shower. And food." She had no more than said the words than her t-shirt was replaced with a clean, pink nightshirt. Zach was still naked, but his hair was dry and his body smelled wickedly masculine, like he'd just left the shower. The sheets beneath them were clean and dry. "Clean-up?" she asked, amused. He really was excellent at cleaning up messes.

"Shower, clean clothes, and sheets done," he replied, his voice laced with humor. "I'll be right back." He lifted her from his lap and set her gently on the clean sheets.

He disappeared before she could blink, and he was back within seconds, his arms full of food from the refrigerator. "It's a good thing that you went shopping so that we actually have food," he commented drily as he returned, dumping the food on the bed and swinging her back into his lap, as though terrified she would disappear.

Most of the food was leftovers, but neither one of them complained as they dined on cold chicken and pizza, washing it down with cans of soda, and shoveling everything in quickly because they hadn't eaten in two days. Other than taking quick trips to the bathroom, Kat hadn't moved from Zach's side.

Once they had their fill, Zach did his demon style clean-up, making everything disappear like it had never been there.

He laid back and pulled her pliant body over his, removing her night-shirt with his magic, sighing as they touched skin to skin. "Jesus. I thought I'd never touch you again." His hands roamed the skin of her back and down to her bare ass, caressing with a firm touch, as though he were trying to reassure himself that she was still with him.

His fear was nearly palpable, still so thick in the air around them that Kat speared her fingers into his hair and kissed him. It was meant to be a kiss of comfort, but his mouth instantly seized hers, his tongue taking control as he nearly kissed the breath from her body. A masculine groan rumbled in his chest and he flipped them over, his lips never leaving hers as he wedged his big body between her thighs.

*Don't ever leave me, Kat. I won't survive it.*

The voice in her head was demanding, yet pleading. Zach plundered her mouth as though he couldn't get enough of her, and she wrapped her legs around his waist, needing him inside her. She put her heels on his ass, trying to nudge him to enter her already wet flesh, but he kept on kissing her, devouring her with his tongue, mimicking what he wanted to do with his cock as his hand ran up and down her sides, his fingers grazing over her skin, leaving goose bumps on her flesh wherever he touched. Her need for him becoming urgent, she thrust her hips up, trying to get him to fill her. "Zach. Please." She needed him so badly, her whole body craving the union of their flesh after their two-day ordeal.

Lifting his mouth from hers, he brushed his lips over her face, her hair, her neck, and taking extra time to run his tongue over her mating mark. "I'm going to make love to you, Kat. And I'm going to savor every second that I'm inside you, possessing you, taking what's mine. I need it and so do you. My body burns for you, but that's only part of how much I need you, and I need more than just your body."

He wanted her to surrender, to give him all of her. And there was nothing she wanted more. The small sliver of his soul that rested inside her thrummed with heat, spreading outward and fusing more tightly with the rest of her soul, and the warmth that spread over her body was electrifying.

Zach moved lower, his lips and teeth worrying her nipples, first one and then the other, bringing a needy moan to her lips that she released in a rush. "Oh God. Zach. I need you."

"You have me, sweetheart," he replied huskily against her breast. Sliding up her body, his mouth to her ear, he added, "I'll never let you go."

His cock slid slowly into her, filling her to capacity inch by inch. He was making love to her, and she shivered with the ecstasy of belonging to him as he buried himself to the hilt. One of his strong arms curled under her ass, cupping it with his hand and keeping her steady for his taking. Her hands fisted in his hair as she felt their intimate connection-body, heart, and soul.

"Look at me. I want to watch you when you come," he demanded as he brushed the hair from her face, his amber gaze searing her as she met his eyes. Their eyes locked as he pumped into her, each stroke a branding, another soul-deep connection that joined them together forever.

His thrusts became more urgent, more demanding, but his eyes never left hers. At that moment, he was the master, and Kat could do nothing but submit. She gasped and moaned as each deep, steady pump of his cock nearly made her come undone. She fell into him, drowned in his eyes, as his intense gaze watched her.

"I love those needy noises you make for me," he rasped, his face fierce as he palmed her ass harder, bringing her throbbing clit against his pubic bone with every hard entry of his cock. "Only for me."

"Yes. I love you, Zach. So much." The words sprung from her mouth naturally as every part of her being fused with his as she shattered, her climax shooting through her body with startling force.

"That's it. Need me. Come for me," Zach rumbled, his eyes holding hers as she shuddered and released a throaty moan.

Kat's eyes were glued to his, her channel spasming around his cock as her orgasm continued to rock her body. Zach pulled his hand out from under her ass, using both hands to hold her head in place, keeping her immobile as he buried himself inside her again and again. He was opening himself to her, letting her see how she affected him as he released a masculine, tortured groan while his scorching release flooded her womb. At that moment, they were both lost in each other, their eyes locked, every part of them combined.

Zach rolled to her side, pulling her until she was half sprawled over him, her head on his chest. Kat couldn't move, breathing heavily as her sated body went limp on top of Zach. His lovemaking had been so intense that she was drained…but in a good way.

"What happened to Kristoff?" Zach asked aloud.

Still trying to recover her breath, she answered him with her mind. *He said he'd be okay. His reaction was less intense. I'm sure he'll come by soon.*

"We need to go back to the demon realm to try to rescue those women," Zach answered fiercely.

"No." Kat sat up and looked at Zach's face as she spoke. "You are not going back. There's nothing you can do. You know you don't have any power there and you'll suffer the consequences. Not even Kristoff can get them out. He said the time will come when they can be rescued."

"I need to go," he snapped at her.

"Fine. Good luck getting back into the demon realm because I'm not taking you. I'm not taking any Sentinels until they have a chance of actually rescuing those women. I won't be responsible for people dying because you're being pigheaded. It makes no sense, Zach." Exasperated, she sat up and glared at him.

"I'll find a way in. I need to go," Zach said impatiently, his jaw tight and his face strained.

"Why are you being so damn stubborn?" Kat sniped at him, irritated. Talking to Zach right now was like talking to a brick wall. And she was so damn tired. She hadn't slept for two days.

"Sleep," Zach answered, his voice suddenly concerned. "We'll talk in the morning."

Kat turned her back to him and laid her head on the pillow, truly angry with him. "You mean you'll order and you'll expect me to do what you want. Well, I won't. Going back into the demon realm is suicide for a Sentinel right now."

Zach released a frustrated sigh as he moved closer to her and curled his arms around her waist protectively. "It's who I am, Kat. My demon instinct is screaming at me."

"You don't always have to be ruled by your nature. I know you can do the right thing, even if it goes against your instincts. This is common sense." Even though she was still angry, her body relaxed, her energy completely drained. She couldn't take anymore.

Kat heard Zach mumble something under his breath, but she didn't have the strength to listen to his thoughts or ask him to repeat what he said.

Within moments, she was asleep.

# Chapter Fourteen

*She's gone.*

Zach could feel the emptiness in every room of his sprawling mansion. It was as if the life had been sucked out of the residence without Kat's presence.

He rubbed his chest as he felt the physical ache of her absence. He got up and poured himself another drink and sank onto the couch in which he'd reclined while Kat had brought him to ecstasy with her mouth.

Breathing in deep, he tried to catch her scent, some remnant of her presence. It was fading. She had just left this morning, and already the emptiness was clawing ruthlessly at his insides, leaving him bleeding and raw.

She had left behind every article of clothing he had gotten for her, all of the cosmetics…anything that he had purchased during her stay. It was as if she didn't want anything he had to give her…including his heart. She had briskly told him that she wouldn't touch a dime of the money that he had put in her account, so he might as well remove it.

Zach had been so destroyed by her actions that he had blocked their mental communication, leaving it open only enough to know she was safe. He didn't want to hear her rejection, or how she was thinking about getting back to her old life as soon as possible. Her hustling out of the door to the waiting taxi she had called, without so much as a fond farewell, had annihilated him.

Every demon instinct he had told him to go after her, throw her over his shoulder and bring her back to him. But damn, humanity could be a real bitch. He wanted her to be with him by choice, and she had chosen to leave. Still, he was seriously considering going demon on her and dragging her back. Really, it was just a matter of time. The demon wanted his *radiant* back, and the man couldn't survive without her. His pride be damned. He wouldn't last another hour, although he wanted to think he could.

"I can't decide whether you're a complete moron or a masochist." Kristoff's deep, sarcastic voice jolted Zach out of his thoughts.

He scowled at his king as Kristoff poured himself a glass of Zach's best Scotch and seated himself in a comfortable recliner across from Zach. "Is no place sacred to you?" Zach grumbled as Kristoff made himself comfortable.

"No. Not when one of my Sentinels is acting like an imbecile," he remarked casually as he took a sip of the perfectly aged whiskey before adding, "Did you or did you not let your *radiant* leave when she was angry with you?"

Zach felt his anger rising as he said, "She didn't want to be with me. Her ass was gone the moment we argued. She claimed she was in love with me, but she still left me."

Kristoff raised a golden brow as he replied, "Even after you told her you loved her?" He shrugged. "Or maybe you don't love her. You didn't want her?"

"I want her. I love her," Zach blurted out emphatically. He took a deep breath before adding, "And I didn't tell her I love her."

Kristoff shook his head at Zach. "She's miserable. You're miserable-"

"She's miserable?" Zach hated that thought. "How do you know?"

"She's under our protection. I checked in on her tonight before I came to knock some sense into your head."

"How do you know she's not happy? She hates it when people read her thoughts," Zach demanded. Honestly, it was more the fact that he hated anyone reading Kat's thoughts except him…but he wasn't going to admit it. Not out loud anyway.

"I'm king. I didn't need to probe her mind to know she was unhappy," Kristoff stated smoothly and without arrogance, as if he were just stating a fact. "Besides, she was crying with her sister and she mumbles to herself when she's alone."

Zach cracked a small grin. "I know." Her mumbled conversations with herself were actually pretty adorable.

"She kept muttering something about being in love with a stupid demon who didn't want her or respect her," Kristoff continued. "When I heard the 'stupid demon' part, I was pretty sure that was you," he finished in a wry tone.

Zach's heart dropped into his stomach. His Kat was crying? Shit. He couldn't bear the thought of her seeing even a moment of unhappiness in her life. "Do you think she really loves me?" he asked Kristoff sheepishly. She'd been pretty pissed at him when she left, not bothering to mention when or if she was coming back.

"Either that or she's been making time with another demon…which I highly doubt," Kristoff answered as he looked at Zach like his Sentinel was a simpleton.

"Did you know before you sent me on this mission that she was my *radiant*?" Zach wondered aloud.

"I knew she was a Sentinel's *radiant* and she definitely wasn't mine. I admit that I suspected as much." Kristoff's answer was careful and evasive.

Zach was doubtful about the "suspected" part. He was fairly certain that Kristoff had known, but was unwilling to admit it. There was plenty that his demon king didn't share. "Why did you come to me and recruit me, Kristoff? I was young. I wasn't your usual type of recruit."

"Some things are fated, Zach," he said abruptly, his expression aloof. His reasons were obviously something he didn't want to discuss in detail. "We were both in the same place at the same time. You needed rescuing. Let's leave it at that for now."

Zach silently cursed his king's mysterious answers. Kristoff liked to play the badass demon king sometimes, but Zach knew better. "I never really thanked you for that. I should have." He would have been homeless in the street and probably dead soon after, had Kristoff not come to him. He'd been too bitter to thank Kristoff before, but now he was ready to say, "Thank you. For everything. You took me into your home and taught me everything I needed to know to be a Sentinel. You didn't have to. You could have found someone older. Someone better," Zach muttered, knowing that after two centuries, it really was time to thank his rescuer. What had happened to Sophie wasn't Kristoff's fault...yet he had blamed him.

"You were bitter. I understood," Kristoff answered wisely. "You might try my patience sometimes, but the investment of my time was completely worth it. You're a good Sentinel, Zach, and a loyal friend. You've served well. It's time for you to be happy."

"Kat doesn't want me to go after the human captives in the demon realm or to say anything to anyone. I'm a Sentinel. My duty is to rescue those people," Zach grumbled. "We argued and she finally left. She said I was being completely unreasonable and if I wanted to go on a suicidal mission, she didn't want to watch me kill myself."

Kristoff tossed back a mouthful of Scotch before asking, "And were you?"

Zach frowned as his eyes rose to Kristoff's face with a questioning look. "Was I what?"

"Were you unreasonable? Did you listen to her? I don't think Kat is the type of woman to just fly off the handle for no reason. And she's right. We don't have the power right now to be able to rescue those humans. You just don't want to admit it," Kristoff replied, leaning back in his chair and continuing to stare at Zach with a dry look. "Do you really want to alert your brothers so you can all go off on a suicide mission? It won't help those women. There is no way to remove them. They're under a bargain with an Evil. Their rescue will take planning and power."

Zach swallowed hard, the reality of the situation finally beating him over the head with a sledgehammer. "So they'll continue to suffer? We'll never be able to get them out?" he asked in a husky voice.

"Not exactly. I think we will be able to help them, but not right now," Kristoff answer cagily.

Zach raised a brow, wondering what his king wasn't sharing with him. "So why do you think that it might be possible in the future if it isn't right now?"

His leader's eyes shifted, no longer looking at Zach, and he sighed heavily. "Do you trust me, Zach?"

"Yes," he answered immediately. Kristoff had never once, in two centuries, given Zach a reason *not* to trust him. In fact, he was heavily in his debt.

"Then let it go for now. There are some things that I can't share because I don't know the whole situation myself. I only know that the opportunity will present itself for us to be able to rescue those women. I know it makes you edgy and restless not to go, but it would be certain death for you, Hunter, and Drew. Trust that as soon as we can accomplish the mission, it will be done."

"Kat was right. I should have listened to her," Zach mumbled, cringing as he remembered the angry and hurt look on Kat's face as she had left that morning. "She doesn't usually get angry. Not really."

"She's afraid. Her fear for you made her angry because she couldn't reach you," Kristoff said philosophically. "Maybe you need to learn to be a little more flexible. Compromise. Think about what you have to lose before you act like an idiot," Kristoff suggested. "Try talking to her instead of giving her ultimatums."

"I'm not sure she'll talk to me." Zach wavered between the desire to go and claim his woman and the need to see her happy.

"Don't start," Kristoff warned. "I know you think you aren't worthy of her, but there has never been a woman more perfect for you, and you deserve her. If being with you wasn't her ultimate happiness, she wouldn't be your *radiant*. She loves you. Don't blow this, Zach. She needs you every bit as much as you need her. Kat hasn't had an easy life. You can change that for her, give her back the love she gives so unselfishly to everyone else."

Even as Kristoff uttered the words, Zach knew he wanted to love Kat that way, give her everything she needed, protect her from anyone and everything that could hurt her. He already did love her that way...but he hadn't told her. He hadn't been fair to her earlier, and he had wounded her. *God, that hurt.* He had thrown away a miracle because of his own stubbornness. "I need to see her." But he was beyond need, his urge more like desperation. "I hope to hell she'll forgive me."

"She will," Kristoff answered smugly. "Charm her."

Zach scowled. "I don't exactly feel like Prince Charming when I'm around her. She makes me crazy. I feel more like the big, bad wolf that wants to gobble her up," he rumbled, his thoughts wandering to their intimate lovemaking the night before, an experience that had been one of the most extraordinary moments of his life. "Will it get easier for me with her?" Zach asked, his deep voice betraying a trace of vulnerability.

Kristoff shrugged. "Probably not. But you'll get used to the feeling," he answered thoughtfully. "Being a dominant asshole is a Sentinel trait. But you can learn to deal with it."

Zach stood, suddenly anxious to get to Kat. He needed to see her so badly that he could barely function. "Is she at her sister's house?"

"She was. When I checked in on her, she was about to head for home. I'm assuming that meant her apartment," Kristoff replied, not bothering to rise as he looked up at Zach and took another sip of Scotch.

"Thanks," Zach said gruffly. "I'll catch you later."

Kristoff waved him off. "Go find your *radiant*. And try talking to her this time. You might want to just mention the fact that you love her," he advised sarcastically.

Zach nodded once, determined to let Kat know exactly how he felt, insecurities be damned. He needed her, and he would make her happier than anyone else on earth could, because no one would ever love her as much as he did.

He transported without another word, his thoughts completely fixed on Kat, leaving Kristoff still seated in his den, a half-empty drink in his hand.

"Don't mind me. I'll just finish my drink and see myself out," Kristoff muttered aloud in the empty den as he tipped his glass up with a sly grin on his face.

"Damn it!"

Kat cursed as she entered another wrong total into her expense report that she kept on her relic of a computer. She got up from her wobbly chair that had seen much better days and went to her compact kitchen to get a bottle of water. As she rummaged through her refrigerator, she realized that she needed to clean it out. Everything was spoiled from disuse with her being gone for over a week.

Her week with Zach.

"Get him out of your head, Kat," she mumbled. "He doesn't want you. He didn't even make a protest about you leaving. Did you really think he would?" She grabbed a bottle of water, ignoring the other items that were beyond rescue. She'd take them out to the trash later.

Returning to her computer, she plopped in the chair and shut the system down for the night. She wasn't accomplishing anything. The chair creaked ominously as she leaned against the loose backrest and opened her water, taking a large swig.

She wanted to go home…to Zach. Okay, she was being stubborn, but she so wasn't going to help him kill himself. Instinct was already clawing at her to return to him, try to talk to him. But her demon didn't talk…he demanded, and there was no way she could keep her temper in check when he was contemplating something as idiotic as going back to the demon realm, nor was she going to help him do it.

"This apartment is depressing." It wasn't just the shabby atmosphere, it was also the silence.

She had always lived on a tight budget and she was used to the secondhand items and never spending hard-earned cash on anything she could live without. Previously, she had spent the money on Stevie. Now she was trying to save enough cash to go back to school.

The apartment was too empty, too quiet. She missed the sultry, sexy baritone of her Sentinel, and she wondered if he was missing her.

*I might be his radiant, and he might want me because of that attraction, but he never said he loved me.*

"He's not yours, idiot. He has no desire for a partnership and he doesn't respect or listen to you," she muttered aloud, just to hear her voice break the silence. "He's a billionaire demon. Why would he want a full-figured, brassy redhead with no accomplishments to her credit except a business that's barely afloat?"

"Perhaps because he adores her."

Kat jumped as Zach appeared behind her. Her heart started pounding as she stood and turned, her heart in her eyes. He reached for a lock of her hair, letting it slide between his fingers as he continued. "Maybe he loves your bright, shiny hair and lusts after your lush body." She trembled, as he added in a husky voice as their eyes locked together, "Or maybe it's because he can't live without seeing your smile every day." He let her hair slide out of his hand and slid his arms around her, pulling her flush against his muscular body as he finished with a harsh whisper near her ear, "I actually think he's just madly in love with you, Kitten."

She shook her head against his shoulder, her eyes misting with tears. "Please don't play with me, Zach."

"I love you, Kat." He pulled back, his glowing gaze colliding with hers. "I don't want to live without you. I can't live without you."

Oh God. Did she dare believe him? She didn't think she'd survive if he didn't mean it. Leaving him had ripped her heart from her chest, and she was still bleeding.

"I mean it, Kat. I'm sorry about this morning. You were right. I wasn't thinking. I was reacting like a Sentinel demon instead of thinking things through completely. You were trying to be my voice of reason and I didn't listen." He sighed heavily before continuing, "I realize I'm no prize for you. I can be bossy and highhanded." He cupped her cheek tenderly and caught a lone tear flowing down her face with his thumb. "But despite all my faults, no one will ever love you as much as I do. I guarantee you that. Stay with me for eternity, Kat. Fight with me if you have to, but don't run away. My life won't be worth a shit if you don't," he finished, his low voice broken and fierce.

Another tear fell, and Kat trembled as she looked up at Zach. "You never said you loved me. I was afraid for you. I shouldn't have left. It was cowardly, but I was so afraid."

"Afraid of me?" he asked, his eyes betraying his sorrow.

"No, afraid *for* you. I didn't want to see you go on a suicide mission and I was scared of how I felt about you. It frightens me. I've never needed someone like this before," she admitted quietly, ashamed of herself for bolting. "I won't run away again, but I won't be silent either when I think you're being unreasonable," she warned him.

"I don't want you to be. I want you exactly as you are," he agreed readily, his eyes devouring her. Kat melted.

*Will I ever get used to the way he looks at me like I'm the only woman on earth for him?*

"Get used to it. You are," he answered as his lips captured hers in a toe-curling, panty-drenching kiss that robbed her of breath and accelerated her heartbeat until it felt like her heart was ready to burst from her chest.

Finally, as he came up for air, he nipped her bottom lip gently and soothed it with his tongue. "Know that if you do run again, I'll be hot on your trail. I've decided that I'm the man who can make you happier than any other," he informed her arrogantly.

Kat stifled a grin. "Is that so?"

"Yes. I have you for eternity so I'll have forever to work on it. I figure I'll get it right eventually."

Kat sighed and laid her head on his muscular chest, listening for a moment as his heart raced in time with hers. "You already have my heart, demon. I don't think you could make me any happier than I am right now."

"Don't bet on it," he returned instantly with a growl.

Kat smiled weakly as her tears were absorbed by the soft cotton of his t-shirt. "Take us home, Zach. I need to get naked and horizontal with you."

"Don't know if I can wait that long. I think it's going to be vertical against the nearest wall," he said huskily.

She laughed with delight as they disappeared. She was leaving the remnants of her old life behind to embark on a new life with the man she loved.

Zach didn't wait, and when the two of them arrived back in his bedroom, he showed her exactly how much he loved her, and it was indeed…vertical.

# Epilogue

One week later, Kristoff sat at Zach's home, watching Kat as she fussed over Hunter's ravaged face, giving the Sentinel a stern lecture about following the rules. To his credit, Hunter didn't growl at her. Instead, he appeared to be listening, even though Kristoff knew it wouldn't change Hunter's behavior. He was humoring his new sister-in-law, the woman who had married his brother in a small private ceremony in the courthouse a few hours ago. Zach looked on from the couch, gritting his teeth every time his mate touched his brother, tolerating it, but just barely. Kristoff shouldn't be amused by Zach's discomfort, but he couldn't help himself. He was, after all, unmated and probably always would be. If he hadn't found his *radiant* by now, she either didn't exist or she had died before he had discovered her. But along with his amusement, he couldn't help but feel a tiny bit of envy. What would it be like to have that sort of connection with a woman?

The frown faded from Zach's face and Kat quit fussing over Hunter as her nephew burst into the room from the kitchen, heading directly for Zach and clambering into a position beside his new uncle on the couch. It was obvious that Zach adored Stevie, and he smiled broadly now, a grin that Kristoff had never seen before, as he ruffled the boy's hair affectionately. Hunter crouched beside the boy and spoke to him in a gentle voice, something else Kristoff had never heard before. Kat deposited herself in her new husband's lap and joined the conversation.

"The Winstons are adding to their family," Drew remarked, his chair right beside Kristoff's. "He's a good kid."

"You adore him. I know you actually shared your favorite truffles with him," Kristoff answered, knowing Drew rarely shared when it came to his favorite foods.

Drew shrugged. "He's a hard kid not to like. He's been through a lot."

Kristoff wasn't fooled for a moment. Hunter and Drew practically worshipped Kat and were incredibly fond of her nephew, as was Zach. They had accepted them all into the Winston fold, including Nora and her husband, Dean, who were currently out getting the cake for the impromptu reception they were having.

Zach had wanted a huge wedding, but Kat had wanted a quiet celebration with just family, and Zach had given in to her wishes.

*I just want you to be mine in every possible way.* Kristoff grinned as he remembered Zach's blunt words when he had finally agreed to marry Kat in any manner she desired.

Tearing his eyes away from the happy couple, Kristoff looked at Drew. "Any luck on finding our anonymous author, or is he still eluding you?"

Drew frowned as he answered. "Yeah. Except I don't think it's a *he*-I think it's a female."

Kristoff tried to feign surprise, but he really...wasn't. "Have you approached her yet?"

"No," Drew answered irritably. "She's wily. I think she actually knows we're looking for her and disappears before I can catch up with her. But now that I'm fairly certain I have her identity pinned down, I'll go after her tomorrow."

Kristoff could tell that it really galled his Sentinel to be outwitted by a human female. "I'm sure you'll take care of it." Okay...it really wasn't easy not to smile. Drew might be the most rational of the three brothers, but he was seriously annoyed by one human female, and knowing the woman who was irritating Drew, Kristoff knew it would only get worse.

His attention diverted by the return of Nora and Dean, Kristoff rose as Kat called them all over to the dining room table for a toast, with Drew following close behind.

As he accepted a glass of champagne, he watched Zach with Kat, the boy he once knew now a man, and he thanked the gods that he had found Zach in time to save him. He hadn't known then exactly why he needed to save the ragged young man who had lived such a rough childhood. Now…he understood. Not only was Zach special because he was an exceptional recruiter, but his *radiant* harbored a skill that had been missing from the Sentinels' arsenal of defense forever. Kat was one key to the lock they needed to open in order to rescue humans who were suffering in the demon realm, some of whom had been there for hundreds of years. Unfortunately, the door had several locks, but they were one step closer to victory. And if the visions that Athena had been having recently were correct, the next lock would give shortly.

He looked from Zach to Drew, and finally to Hunter. In every way but blood, these men were his kin, closer to him than any other of his Sentinels, the three men he trusted to have his back when he needed them. Although the Sentinels hadn't been created to form relationships and develop emotions, they had, and they were so much more than the emotionless warriors that the gods had originally created. He'd been through the evolution, and although it might have been easier to remain as he'd been in the beginning, that had been an empty existence.

"To love, happiness, and family," Zach's loud baritone rang out as they all raised their glasses.

Kristoff's heart lifted as the happy couple embraced and touched their flutes together, and then reached out for everyone else. He made sure he tapped every single glass in the room, because he certainly could drink to that toast.

## ~The End~

Look for Drew's story, *A **Dangerous Hunger***,
coming in February 2014.

## Please visit me at:

http://www.authorjsscott.com
http://www.facebook.com/authorjsscott

You can write to me at jsscott_author@hotmail.com

You can also tweet @AuthorJSScott

Made in the USA
Lexington, KY
20 July 2016